ORIGINS

THE WASTELAND CHRONICLES BOOK 2

KYLE WEST

RAGNAROK PRESS

ALSO BY KYLE WEST

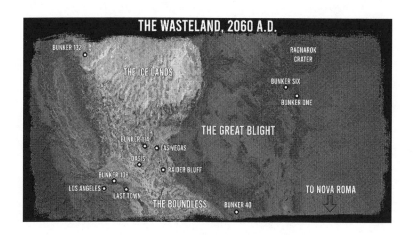

ONE

W e had left Bunker 114 and Cold Mountain behind hours ago and darkness cloaked the Wasteland. As we sped east toward Raider Bluff, I wondered if Brux's parting shot meant our mission had failed before it could even begin.

Samuel's eyes remained closed for almost the entire journey. Wet blood soaked his right shoulder. The congealer had slowed the bleeding somewhat, but still, he wouldn't last for long. There was no exit wound, meaning the bullet was still inside. If we didn't find Char fast enough, either Makara or I would have to remove it.

The Recon's bright blue lights pushed back the night, letting us see ahead in a wide arc. Thirty years of dust covered most parts of the highway. We zoomed past decrepit buildings, ghost towns, and mangled road signs, as we pushed on toward our goal.

Makara sped as fast as the heavy Recon would go – about fifty-five miles per hour, the wheels churning to get us to our destination.

I just didn't know if it was fast enough.

When the highway turned south, a wide dark river became visible on our left, flowing south.

"We hit the Colorado," Makara said. "It won't be long, now."

It was more water than I'd ever seen in my life. I'd read about the Colorado River in the Bunker 108 archive. It had once been an important river in the Old World, but overuse had dried it up. Now the river was wide – so wide, in fact, that I couldn't see the other side in the darkness. Above the river on the opposite bank, high up, rose Raider Bluff. The city's yellow lights glowed dimly with distance.

At last, the road turned left, toward the river, where a bridge of tall arches spanned the water.

"Silver Arched Bridge," Makara said. "The only bridge the Raiders have kept up for miles."

The giant rungs of the arch stretched from shore to shore with the road running straight underneath. Two Raiders with rifles guarded the bridge's front, shielding their eyes against the Recon's headlights.

"Let me do the talking," Makara said.

We pulled up, and Makara rolled down the window.

A hard-faced, grizzled man peered inside. His eyes widened as he saw who was driving.

"Makara?"

"Chris, step aside. I have a wounded man in here who will die without medical attention."

"What?" Chris asked. He shined the flashlight inside the Recon, pointing the beam at Makara, Samuel, and then me. "What happened? Where's Brux? Twitch? Tyson?"

"All dead. Let me through. I don't have time for these questions!"

"What happened?"

"Gunshot wound," Makara said, with a growl.

"Now step aside. Call ahead for Char. Let him know I'm coming."

"Not so fast," he said. "I'm not putting my ass on the line until you answer some questions. First, who is this?"

He pointed at me.

"Look, Chris," Makara said, "Just give me clearance to Char or I'll have him wipe the floor with you. I promise, you not listening to me is more dangerous than this sixteen-year-old kid and a man dying from a gunshot wound."

Chris's gaze was doing its best to match up with Makara's, but in the end, she was the victor. He turned away and raised his radio to his mouth.

"HQ...Makara's back. I'm sending her up. Have the gates ready, over."

"Copy that," a voice said from the other end.

"Welcome home, Makara," Chris said sarcastically. "You're clear. I hope you have a better story for Char than you do for me."

"I don't need a story, Chris." Makara said.

Makara was about to gun the accelerator when Chris grabbed her shoulder.

"What now?" she asked, shrugging off his grasp.

"Be careful up there. Things have changed. An emissary from the Empire is in Bluff, talking with Char."

"The Empire?" Makara asked. "What the hell is the Empire?"

Chris frowned. "You were gone longer than I thought. They're based in Old Mexico. They're big, powerful – tens of thousands of people." He paused. "The emissary's name is Rex. Just don't get on his bad side. I know you can be mouthy."

Makara shook her head. "I'll say what I want, *when* I want. Is that it?"

"Yeah. You should head on. Just watch your back."

Makara didn't waste any more words on him. When Chris stepped aside, Makara floored the Recon, rocketing into the night.

"The Empire," I said. "That sounds sinister."

"I've never heard of it before," Makara said. "Gone a few months, and this is what happens. The game always changes every time I come back."

"It's hard to imagine war at a time like this," I said. "The world is being taken over by the xenovirus. Leave it to humanity to take itself out first."

Makara sighed. "All the more reason to patch my brother up and be on our way. We have a mission to finish."

I looked at Samuel, who was still out like a light. His chest rose and fell evenly, so there was at least that...but for how much longer?

"Just a few minutes, Sam," Makara said. "Hang on."

WE DROVE UP WHAT SEEMED TO BE AN ENDLESS SERIES OF switchbacks before the land leveled and placed us before the wooden gates of Raider Bluff. These things were huge, at least twenty-five feet high. They made the gates of Oasis look like toys in comparison. A giant wooden palisade surrounded all sides of the town, maybe twenty feet high, as if the sheer cliffs weren't enough. It must have taken an eternity to build all this. I wondered where the Raiders had found the labor, until I remembered that Raiders were notorious for employing slaves.

At various points in the perimeter, large watchtowers rose. I wondered where they had gotten the lumber to build these walls. Trees were still growing *somewhere*, apparently, if not here.

The gates drew back, sliding into the walls on either

side. Thick chains rigged to pulleys moved the massive fortifications. Even though I was about to enter the biggest den of thieves in the entire world, I couldn't help but be impressed.

Makara drove down the main drag. Wooden buildings and saloons lined either side of the dirt road. It was like entering an Old West town on steroids. Signs swung above the open doors – liquor, girls, and guns seemed to be the establishments' main themes, and electricity powered multicolored neon signs, probably scrapped from nearby cities. Raiders dressed in dingy apparel flanked both sides of the road, making way as we came in. From their widened eyes, it was clear that none of them had expected a Recon, or much less had even *seen* one.

The Raiders tried to get the Recon to stop, but Makara honked the horn which emanated with a low, echoing bellow, which caused them to scatter. She only sped up when they got too close.

"They're not going to hurt us," she said. "They just want to check out the ride."

Outside, I could hear them yelling her name.

"You seem to be pretty popular around here," I said.

"Yeah, something like that."

The road wound its way around the mesa. We weren't even close to the top. There were three levels, and buildings rose from all of them. The bottom, which we were on, was by far the largest. It seemed to contain all the places of business, the wide outdoor markets, the bars, housing, or pretty much anywhere you could buy something.

"We're heading to the Alpha's Compound," Makara said. "It's where Char lives. It's at the very top of Bluff and exclusive. No one will bother us there. Char, in addition to being the Alpha, is also good at stitching a wound. Hopefully, this isn't beyond his expertise."

"You said before that Char is a good man?"

Makara nodded. "Probably the only one who passes for decent around here. It's a wonder he's still alive."

We entered the second level, meaning we were halfway up the bluff. On either side were well-constructed wooden cabins.

Makara pointed out a small building we drove by. A sign overhung the door, reading "The Bounty."

"That's the Bounty," Makara said. "It's a bar run by my friend Lisa. I've spent many-a-night there."

We rounded the last bend. Over the wooden rooftops of Bluff spread the vast panorama of dark desert. The black Colorado River flowed south and the sky above was dark and void.

We reached a final gate. A Raider pulled it open from the other side, revealing a long cobblestone road that led into a grassy courtyard. The green grass must have been watered and well-cared for to flourish like that. Flanking either side of the road were tall pines. I rolled down my window, the trees' crisp, sweet smell filling my nostrils. The stone structure of the compound was a U-shape, surrounding the courtyard. It had narrow slits for windows. Ahead, the cobblestone drive ended in a cul-de-sac. A wide yet short stairway led to a pair of heavy wooden doors. Judging from the thick stone walls, the compound had been constructed to withstand an all-out siege.

"Fancy," I said.

"It's grown over the last few years," Makara said. "Each new Alpha leaves his own mark. Char redid the courtyard. The pines were taken from mountains far to the east."

"Why is he called Char?" I asked.

Makara smiled grimly. "You'll see."

Makara pulled to a stop. She powered off the Recon,

the hum of the hydrogen pressure tank dimming to nothing.

We hopped out of the vehicle. The air was dry, cold, and sharp. It had definitely dropped a few degrees. We went to Samuel's side and opened the passenger's door. Makara and I lifted him from the Recon.

He stirred a bit and groaned. Despite the sound he'd made, his whole body was limp. He was dead weight between us.

"Come on," Makara said. "We're going to have to drag him."

We dragged him through the compound, to the large front doors. Makara didn't bother knocking. She threw the doors open with her shoulder, revealing a wide, dark interior lit by torches. We dragged Samuel inside.

"Char!" Makara yelled.

No one answered her call, which echoed into silence. The entry hall was empty, lit only by two blazing braziers along the far wall and a few torches ensconced upon the four heavy pillars supporting the room's structure.

A shadow materialized in front of us, moving forward at lightning speed.

"Watch out!" I said.

Makara reached for her handgun with her free hand, never letting go of Samuel.

A thin, curved sword was placed at the base of Makara's neck.

"Not so fast," a young, female voice said.

TWO

Standing in the light, the bearer of the sword was revealed to be a black-haired girl, about my age, with green almond eyes. The eyes narrowed as she edged the blade closer to Makara's throat. I saw that she was beautiful, with a short, yet curvy, figure. I berated myself for even noticing that at a time like this, but even at the threat of one's life, men can't help but notice certain things. I guessed she was about my age, or perhaps a year or two older.

"Who are you," she asked dangerously, "and what are you doing here?"

Makara spoke first, making an effort to keep calm. "We're here to see Char, girl. Put that thing away before you hurt someone."

"Char is not here. And maybe hurting someone is the whole point." The girl did not withdraw her sword. In fact, it looked as if she had a mind to use it. "If you had been cleared, I would be the first to know."

"Chris called ahead," Makara said, losing patience. "I know Char, he and I go way back. Bet you didn't know that, you insufferable..."

"I'll give you one more chance," the girl said. "Tell me who you are, and why you're here. This wouldn't be the first assassination attempt I've stopped."

"I don't know *who* you think you are, but Char and I are old friends." Makara didn't bat an eyelash. "I'm Makara. Ever heard the name? And if you don't get us Char, then..."

The front doors banged open. I turned to see a grizzled man, probably in his fifties, enter, flanked by two bodyguards.

"Makara," he said, his voice gravelly. "You've returned."

The girl paused, unsure, and Makara used her hesitation to step safely away from the blade. The girl frowned, but sheathed her katana with a flourish. All eyes went to Char.

There was no mistaking the man's air of command. He was tall with broad shoulders and a shaved head. Two guards flanked either side, holding rifles. His sharp blue eyes surveyed us calmly. He wore green camo pants and a black leather jacket. A tattoo of a snakelike dragon eating its own tail was emblazoned on his forearm.

His most striking feature, however, was his face. A deep burn wound marred his right cheek. That wound had happened long ago and would never fully heal.

"I'm sorry I wasn't here to greet you," he said to Makara. "Politics. Don't blame my bodyguard for the cold reception. She's only doing her job."

With that, the still nameless girl seemed to relax.

"Her name is Anna," Char said. "She's an expert at the katana. I don't know where she learned to fight like that, but now, she works for me. But we don't have time for introductions, do we?"

Char looked down at Samuel, who lay on the ground between Makara and me.

"Lay him face-up," Char said. "I need to see the wound."

Makara and I flipped him, while Anna watched. Char knelt beside him, placing two fingers on his neck.

He glanced sideways at Makara. "Is the bullet still in?"

"Yes. It happened about four hours ago."

Char pulled Samuel's tee shirt back to reveal the wound. Fresh red blood trickled out. The surrounding skin was black, purple, and green.

"He'll die if I try to pull it out of him like this. He needs morphine."

"You have that, don't you?" Makara asked.

Char grunted. "A bit. With luck, it'll be enough." Char motioned to his bodyguards nearby. "We're taking Samuel to the clinic."

The two men gathered around, and Anna came forward to help. Together, they lifted Samuel up.

"Follow me," Char said to Makara. He seemed to notice me for the first time. "Who are you?"

"Alex," I said.

"He's from Bunker 108," Makara said. "Once we take care of Samuel, we'll fill you in on everything. It's a long, long story."

Char grunted in reply, and said nothing more.

Together, we followed him through the dark corridors of the Alpha's Compound.

CHAR AND HIS MEN SET SAMUEL UP IN A HOSPITAL BED. After washing his hands, Char found a syringe and filled it with a dosage of morphine. He inserted it into Samuel's arm. Samuel gave no reaction.

Slowly, Char pushed down on the syringe.

"It's working," Char said.

Char next took a pair of forceps and began to dig into the open wound. Samuel was completely out. If he had been conscious, that pain would have been near unbearable.

"Do you have medical training?" I asked.

"My training is more of the school of hard knocks than anything else," Char said. "I'm the best in Bluff, that's for sure."

Samuel was still. It was as if he were already dead.

Makara watched, biting her lip. More blood oozed from Samuel's wound, staining his shirt and the sheets. Char dug, using his fingers to widen the puncture. We watched as he searched for the bullet.

A minute later, Char pulled it out.

"It didn't fragment," he said. "Your brother's lucky."

"Will he live?" Makara asked.

"There's no reason why he shouldn't. I just have to clean the wound and stitch him up. Obviously, he'll need to stay in bed for a while and take it easy."

"How long?" Makara asked.

"We can tell better over the next few days," Char said. "The wound could have been a lot worse. If he's lucky, I'll let him out in two weeks. But that's on the short end. It might even be months."

Months? Samuel would never stand for that. He would want to be out of that bed the next day if at all possible.

Char applied some sort of cream to the wound, which slowed the bleeding. He began stitching it shut. Then he grabbed a bottle of clear liquid and daubed it onto the wound. Next, he wrapped the wound tightly with a bandage. Done with that, he washed his hands once more and went to the cabinet. From it he retrieved a sling. He placed it over Samuel's neck and gingerly pulled Samuel's arm through.

"He'll need to wear that for a while. A couple of months, at least, before I'd trust taking it off."

"He'll be fine though, right?" Makara asked.

Char gave a reassuring smile, which did little to soften his hardened face. "I've seen men live through much worse. He should come around in the morning. He'll be in a lot of pain – but the worst of it is over. He just needs to rest, eat, and sleep. I can have Anna stay and watch over him while you guys get some rest."

"No need," Makara said. "I can sit with Samuel."

"No," Char said. "I insist. I have guest bedrooms in the east wing. They are more comfortable than anything you'll find in the city."

"What about the Recon?"

"It'll stay safe out there," Char said. "No one can drive it, anyway."

Makara waited for a moment. She didn't want to leave Samuel with Anna. The two of them had gotten off on the wrong foot, that was for sure.

"Come on, Makara," I said. "He'll be fine."

Makara relented. "All right. I could do with a rest, anyway."

"Anna," Char said, "show them to the guest rooms."

She looked at us. "Follow me."

We left the clinic and walked the empty stone halls. We said nothing more as she led us to the east wing. We stopped before a door.

"This is it," she said. "There's another room just like this one across the hall. You'll find the bathroom and showers down that way."

"Showers?" I asked.

"Yes," she said. "Be sparing with the water. It's a pain to bring up here."

She left us behind, walking back the way she had come. She disappeared into the darkness of the hallway.

"Don't even think about it," Makara said.

I looked at Makara. "What?"

"You know what. I saw how you were looking at her. She's crazy, that one. Just trying to help you, is all."

"I don't know what you mean."

She gave an exasperated sigh, then turned placed a hand on the knob.

"Get some sleep, Alex. We'll be out of here before you know it. You'll see."

She stepped into her room, leaving me alone in the hallway. I opened the door to my own bedroom and slipped inside.

I took off my clothes, and set my Beretta on the nightstand nearby. I wanted that weapon always close.

I meant to take a shower, but instead, I found myself laying down, just for a moment. I was asleep in seconds.

THREE

I woke up with every bone in my body aching and every muscle sore. The last week had been sheer madness. I had lost my home, my entire life, and everyone I cared about. I had wandered alone in the Wasteland and had been chased around by both Raiders and monsters. Somehow I had met Makara and Samuel, and ended up here.

The fact that I was lying in a bed after a week of hell was surreal. It was as if all the sleep in the world wouldn't be enough to melt the weariness from my body.

I fell asleep again, and awoke sometime later. I knew I needed to get up. I had to check on Samuel and find some food, the thought of which set my stomach growling. I hadn't eaten since the morning of the day before.

I got up, both of my legs stiff and sore, as if I were sixty rather than sixteen.

I stepped into the hall and headed for the bathroom. I found it on the left. It was an open room made of gray stone. I stood under one of the two shower heads and let the cold water flow over me. Though the water was cold, feeling the layers of sweat and filth washing off made me feel as if I were a new person. I used a nearby bar of soap to scrub the rest of the grime off. I wasn't happy to see I'd been sleeping with monster and spider bits still caked on my skin.

Once done, I toweled off, grabbed my dirty clothes, and headed back to my room, suppressing shivers.

In my room, there was a mirror beside the door. I looked into it, seeing that I had lost weight. I had been quite skinny to begin with, so it made eating all the more important.

I changed into a clean set of clothes – desert camo pants and a white tee. I would've put on my hoodie, because the air was cool, but the clothing was matted with dirt and the horror show that had been Bunker 114. I decided to go without it. Hopefully, someone would come by and clean it.

I walked down the hall to the clinic. Now that it was day, I took the opportunity to look around at every-thing. The stonework must have taken a long time to shape and put together. Torches still gave off dancing light at regular intervals along the hallway, adding addi-tional light. The entire building was U-shaped – there were two parallel wings, one of which I was in, connected by the entry hall. I could walk from one end of the wing to the other in about a minute. It obviously wasn't just Char living here – it was his personal guards, cooks, slaves, and guests. It was a massive facility. Part of the building, if not most, might have even existed pre-Ragnarok.

As I made my way to the clinic, I passed the compound's occupants – Raiders with guns, slaves hurrying to clean. It was very different from what I was used to, and it was hard not to feel guilty that the slaves were needed to keep a fortress like this running.

I passed by an open window to see Anna practicing

with her blade in the courtyard under a tall pine. Her movements were quick, fluid, and repetitive. I could hear the blade whirring even from my distance. Her grace and skill were amazing. It was hard not to stand there and watch, because it was clear her constant work-outs had honed her body of any extraneous fat while giving her a toned and shapely form. Though she was small, she had curves that made it very difficult to look away.

I turned from the window to walk to the clinic. When I entered, I found Makara already there.

"Is he awake?" I asked.

Eyes heavy, Makara shook her head. It looked as if she hadn't slept at all.

That was when Samuel's eyes flickered open.

"Sam?" Makara asked.

"Hey, Makara."

His voice was parched. Makara reached for a glass of water nearby and held it to his lips.

"How are you feeling?" Makara asked.

Samuel took a swallow of water. He took too much, though; he coughed and winced in pain.

"Easy," Makara said. "There's no rush."

"Where am I?"

"We're in Char's compound," Makara said. "We made it to Raider Bluff. He saved your life."

Samuel closed his eyes. I could not tell if it was out of relief or dread. He opened them again, and turned his head to the window. He stared at the red clouds outside.

"Are you hungry?" Makara asked.

"Yeah. I could eat."

"I have a servant getting us food, so she should be back soon."

Samuel closed his eyes again. "You mean *slave?*"

Makara shrugged. "They are one and the same

here." She paused a moment. "That was a nasty shot you took."

"I just hope it doesn't keep us long."

"We need to rest to recoup our strength a bit, anyway. I talked to Char, and he's fine with us staying as long as we need." She hesitated. "Even through the winter."

"We've got to leave as soon as we can," Samuel said. "You know that. It's already October. The first snows will have fallen in Cheyenne. A month from now, the land will be impassable."

"It's that cold there?" I asked.

"Colder than you realize," Samuel said. "The world is much colder than it used to be, because of Ragnarok. The world now stands at the dawn of a new Ice Age."

Samuel coughed, and Makara put more water to his lips. He drank.

"Don't strain yourself, Samuel," Makara said.

Samuel settled back into his pillow. "If anything happens, you'll have to go on without me."

"Don't say that," Makara said. "That's not going to happen. We'd be useless without you."

Samuel didn't respond. He only closed his eyes.

A middle-aged woman with dark brown hair walked in, carrying a tray that held a large pot of stew, wooden bowls, spoons, and a plate stacked thickly with flat-bread. The steaming pot gave off a spicy, savory aroma that set my stomach growling. She set the tray on an end table. She left the room, her footsteps fading down the hallway.

"It's awful," I said. "Slavery."

Makara took a bowl, and filled it with stew, not looking too concerned. "It is what it is."

"I know I can't change anything. It's just that this world is a lot harsher than I thought."

Makara took the bowl of stew, not for herself, but for Samuel. She pulled up her chair beside him.

"Makara, no," he said. "I can handle this."

"Samuel, don't be stubborn. You only have one good hand, so you'll spill it."

"No, I won't." He glared at her. "Hand me that bowl."

Makara held onto it. "If you want to eat, it will be with me feeding you."

"Makara..."

She arched an eyebrow.

Seeing he was not going to win, Samuel sighed. "Fine."

Taking that as a sign of her victory, Makara jabbed the spoon into the bowl and forced it to Samuel's lips. He begrudgingly took a bite.

I helped myself to the stew, which had a reddish-brown hue. It was filled with potatoes, carrots, onions, leeks, and tomatoes, along with small cuts of meat. After filling my bowl, I chowed down, not minding how hot it was. The stew was thick, dark, and filling.

"What kind of meat is this?" I asked.

"Camel," Makara said.

I nearly spat the food back out. *"Camel?"*

I had never even considered that camel could be eaten – though it would make sense, given how numerous they were. The meat was cut into thin slices and was red in the center. It was tough, like jerky.

Despite the strange taste, I decided that camel wasn't *that* bad, though that could have just been my hunger. I filled up a second bowl and ate until I couldn't have another bite.

Anna entered the room, her face covered with a thin sheen of sweat and her katana sheathed on her back. I tried not to focus on how her shirt clung to her curves.

I was surprised when it was me she looked at. "Char wants to see you."

"He wants to see me? What for?"

"You'll find out soon enough. It's best not to keep him waiting."

Anna headed out the door, clearly expecting me to follow.

I looked at Makara. "What does he want?"

"I don't know. I'd get moving if I were you."

"What if he asks about our mission? What do I say?"

"Don't lie," Samuel said. "But at the same time, don't volunteer everything. Remember, he's the most powerful man in the Mojave. Don't make an enemy of him."

"No pressure, then."

"Go, Alex," Samuel said. "Don't keep him waiting."

I walked out of the clinic and followed Anna to the entry hall.

FOUR

Anna led me to Char in the entry hall. He was busy speaking with someone who appeared far more important than me.

The man had a full, black beard, and wore a fine brown cloak with a hood. The clothing and facial hair instantly reminded me of the slavers Makara and I had found on the road a few days ago. I put two and two together and guessed that this man was Rex – the emissary from the Empire...and Char did not look happy to be speaking with him.

Rex was alone. He did not have any bodyguards, or any visible weapons. He either had a lot of gall, or a lot of foolishness.

I waited some twenty feet from their conversation.

"Just think of the possibilities of an alliance between Raider Bluff and the Empire," Rex said. "Already the trade between our peoples ties us economically. Why not further cement that bond with a treaty?"

Char scowled. "Trade, yes. But we Raiders are independent. This is our land, from here to L.A., all the way north to Vegas. And it will always be our land."

Rex smiled, as if he understood that sentiment. "All citizens of the Empire have freedom. Most wish to join us. We offer protection and resources to all our provinces. Raider Bluff would see the same benefits, and who knows? An alliance might see you controlling Las Vegas and Los Angeles as well."

"Yeah, I might control them. But Emperor Augustus would control me."

"You would rule with complete autonomy," Rex continued, never minding Char's point. "Nova Roma is far to the south – if an arrangement could be made, your people would be given a great deal of latitude. There is great wealth to be had by both of us if we were to ally, Char. And now, more than ever, we *need* to ally, with the Blights ever encroaching."

"Yes," Char said. "You say alliance, when I know you mean annexation. That's what happens to any city that 'allies' with you. The Empire does by the knife what it can't do by the pen."

Rex smiled, but his face went dark. "Then we understand each other perfectly."

"You threaten me, in my own home, surrounded by my own men? That's not a mistake most people would make."

Rex smiled thinly, eyes amused. "I'm confident that you are a man of reason, Char. Should anything happen to me, Raider Bluff would be crushed within the year. A single legion of Nova Roma's army could wipe this place from the map. Consider it a great mercy that Augustus chooses not to do so.

"If Augustus desires this blasted desert, then let him come and take it. A man who would give away all he has without a fight is no man at all. Run back to your Emperor and tell him that."

"I was afraid you might say something like that.

That is unfortunate. I will return to Nova Roma immediately."

"Raider Bluff will never become part of the Empire.
We bow to no man, Emperor or not."

Several Raiders flanking the doorway stepped
behind Rex, barring his exit. Rex took a step back,
running right into them.

"I don't think you understand how things work in
the Wasteland. If I were to kill you now, it would be
months before the Emperor were to discover your
absence. Months longer that we can prepare for the
inevitable war."

Rex's face blanched – for the first time, he seemed to
be afraid. There was fear, not superiority, in those eyes.
But he wasn't going to give up.

"If I am not back at Colossus at my appointed time,
you will rue the day you did injury to me. By killing me,
you will make a mortal enemy of the Empire. Your
death will be of the most excruciating kind. This city
will be razed to the ground, and its people slaughtered.
The Empire will empower your enemies, giving great
reward when they do you harm. This will all happen
within a year, as inevitable as the setting of the sun each
day." Rex stepped forward, his last play, but Char
merely expanded his chest, looking down at the smaller
man. "It is not too late to come back. The Empire
doesn't rule with an iron fist; it only desires a small
portion of your wealth. A far better alternative than the
inevitable slaughter that will come, should you reject
my words."

Char barked a laugh. "Let your legions come. Let
them break in an unyielding tide on Raider Bluff's
walls. Let us all die to the last man. But never let us bow
to you or your damn Emperor."

Rex smiled. "Many have said similar words. I look
forward to the day, when the sword is at your neck, that

you beg to take those words back. You would not be the first, Alpha Char of the Raiders."

Char stepped back, nodding to the Raiders who had gathered around him. "What do you think, Raiders?"

"Kill him where he stands," one said. "But slowly."

"Throw him from Vulture Rock!"

"Break his bones, one at a time," another said. "Make him beg to take his *own* words back."

Char chuckled, even as Rex's face whitened. "I like that one the most. But I consider myself a merciful man, and after all, I can see that you're out of your depth."

That was when Char went to Anna, drawing her katana. Rex backed away, face horrified, but he only ran into two Raiders, which grabbed his arms and kept him immobile. His face became venomous.

"You are making a terrible mistake!"

"If the Empire attacks one day," Char said, stepping forward, "you won't live to see it." He swung the blade to within an inch of Rex's neck; the man was now shaking. "You realize I can't let you leave here alive, don't you? You should have come with an army, otherwise you're just wasting your breath."

"The Emperor will learn of this," Rex spat. "And when he does, you will not be joining the Empire as citizens...but as slaves."

With a roar, Char drew the blade back sliced Rex's neck. Rex's eyes widened the moment before the blade made contact, slicing through the flesh and bone. His head flew through the air as a fountain of blood spewed upward. The head bounced off a stone column before hitting the floor, its expression a horrible display of fear and pain. The eyes remained open, staring vacantly ahead.

Char handed the blade to Anna, who, without batting an eye, wiped it on Rex's clothes before sheathing it. Char turned, facing everyone in the room.

"Throw this scum's body off Vulture Rock."

The Raiders nodded and lifted the headless corpse. Another took the head – probably to find a nice pike to stick it on.

I didn't say anything, completely horrified by what I'd just seen. Char was eerily calm, however...a true killer just going about his day's work. A killer who had summoned me to speak to him.

I was thankful to see Makara enter the room from the west wing of the compound. "What the hell is going on?"

Char didn't answer, but Makara saw the Raiders carrying Rex's body and head toward the front doors.

"Who was that?" she asked. "That wasn't Rex, was it?"

Char gave a slow nod. "It's done. There will be war with the Empire."

Makara's face went white. "Char..."

"He wanted to make us slaves," Char said. "And that is something that will never happen."

"Yeah," Makara said. "I can see that now."

"Both of you," Char said, addressing me as well, "follow me. Since you're both here, I might as well make use of you."

"What do you need?" Makara asked.

"Answers." Char gestured toward a long table in front of a fireplace.

We followed him there and sat. It was all I could do to stop myself from shaking at the barbaric display I had just witnessed.

"You've returned alone, with your brother and this boy. What happened to Brux?"

Makara told him everything that had happened – her escape from Brux and the raid group, meeting me, and finding Samuel. She also told him about our mission – to head to Bunker One to discover the origins of the xenovirus, and how we hoped to find a cure for it. It took almost an hour of continuous talking. Char nodded from time to time, and only interrupted with a few questions. At last, Char was up to speed as much as any of us were.

"We have noticed the Blights spreading, obviously," Char said. "There are several growing near here. We have even lost some men to attacks. Monsters that look like lizards with sharp teeth that can run incredibly fast." Char sighed. "The men have taken to calling them 'crawlers.' And there are much worse monsters that have no name, further east. There is also a new kind, called Howlers. They were human once, but these have become something else. They make an awful howling sound when they attack." Char looked at Makara seriously. "I'm afraid that if you go east, you'll find nothing but death, and the further east you go, the worse it gets."

Makara didn't say anything. "We have to go there, Char. It's the only way to learn more about the virus."

"Say you do find the answer. How to cure to the xenovirus. What then?"

Makara shook her head. "I don't know. But we have to try something. Samuel won't stop until he has answers. This is his mission, really. Alex and I are just along for the ride."

Char looked at me, his eyes weighing. "If that's true, there's more to you than meets the eye, Alex."

I wasn't sure what to say to that, so I just added to what Makara had already said. "We need to leave as soon as we can. Winter will be coming on soon, and if what you say about the Blights is true, we'll have to move even faster."

"When you leave these walls," Char said, "you probably won't be coming back."

"Why do you say that?" I asked.

"Even if you make it that far, against all odds, what are the chances you'll make it back?"

I gave no reaction, but it was not something I had given much thought. It made sense, though. It seemed strange to think that we were willingly walking toward our deaths. We might not even make it in the first place.

"We know that," Makara said. "This is what we've decided."

"The only reason I say that is because of the Great Blight," Char said. "The one that starts, and doesn't end."

I frowned. "The Great Blight?"

"Just like it sounds," Char said. "It starts at Ragnarok Crater – or at least I assume it does – and spreads hundreds and hundreds miles outward in each direction. It grows every year – our last patrol reported it starting somewhere a little ways into what used to be New Mexico. It's probably farther west by now."

"If we don't do anything," I said, "one day everything will be the Great Blight...Raider Bluff included."

"That's what I'm afraid of," Char said. "I hate to see you go so soon after getting back, Makara. It's good what you did to Brux, but you should probably keep what really happened between us. Mutiny is mutiny, and someone who has it out for you could make trouble if they found out."

"You think I don't already know that?"

"Just looking out for you, Makara. Who would I be if it wasn't for that?"

Makara nodded, but said nothing. I remembered Makara's story, about how Char had helped her after the Lost Angels had fallen. He was probably the closest thing to a father that she had.

Makara was about to respond when Anna came to the table, her eyes wide.

"What is it?" Char asked.

"Trouble at the Bounty," she said.

Makara stood. "The Bounty? What's happened?

"Some men loyal to the Empire heard about Rex," Anna said. "They're holding Lisa hostage."

"I have to get down there," Makara said, running from the table for the doors.

"Makara!" I said.

But my words went unheeded. Makara only had one thing on her mind.

"Anna, Alex...go with her," Char said. "I'll gather some of my men and meet you down there."

Anna turned to me. "Let's go."

FIVE

Anna and I ran into the courtyard, chasing after Makara, who had already made it past the compound gates. The Bounty wasn't far – maybe half a mile down the winding dirt road.

We ran out the gates and flew down the dirt road past wooden buildings. The streets had emptied a great deal, but what people there were seemed to be heading for the bar. If word had just reached the compound, that meant people around here had known about it for longer.

A few minutes later, we were there. The crooked frame of the Bounty looked as if it were barely holding together. White paint peeled from years of the relentless wind. The front door was wide open, revealing several upturned barstools and glittering broken glass. No sound came from within. It might as well have been abandoned.

Makara had already pushed her way through a small crowd that had gathered outside. She stopped before the front door. Anna and I pushed through the crowd to catch up with her.

"Makara!"

"Look out!" someone yelled from behind.

I looked up to see a man had appeared in the top window, aiming a rifle down at Makara. But instantly, every Raider in the area aimed his gun at the man and shot, the gunfire shocking my senses. The man screamed, slumped from the window and fell, crashing into the dirt below.

"Well, there's one less to deal with," Makara said. "We can't hope any of the others are that dumb."

"What do they even want?" I asked.

"I don't know the whole situation," Anna said, "but somehow Lisa found out that these guys are working with Rex. She raised the alarm, so they ended up taking her hostage. They want out of the town in exchange for her life."

"Char won't let that happen," Makara said. "He doesn't want a single one returning to Colossus to tell the Empire."

"That's what I'm thinking," Anna said.

As if mentioning Char were a summons, I spotted him walking down the road from the direction of the compound, surrounded by a contingent of Raiders. He appeared calm and in control – Makara and I were anything but.

Char approached us. "What's the situation?"

"They're still holed up in there," Anna said. "Two, maybe a few more, on the top floor. They want out of Bluff in exchange for Lisa's life."

Char faced upward. "Okay," he called. "I'm here. What do you want?"

Everyone quieted. Only the wind blew through the dust-strewn street. The people in front of the Bounty began to murmur.

A full minute passed with no response from the bar.

"I demand an answer!" Char bellowed.

"Let us out of here," a voice said. "You know what happens if you don't."

"You kill her, then what?" Char asked. "You die."

"We'll do it if you give us no choice."

"There is no need for that," Char said. "I am glad to let you scum out of my town if it means saving Lisa."

It was quiet. I could imagine the men in that upstairs bedroom, debating quietly on what they should do.

"How can you guarantee our safety?" the same one asked.

"I promise, none of my men will lay a finger on you. I'll have them set down their guns when you come out. We can escort you by Recon, which should protect you if anyone decides to go commando on your sorry asses."

"I never agreed to that," Makara said.

Char held a hand up, silencing her.

The men on the second floor were quiet.

Then: "Have everyone drop their weapons. We agree."

Char scowled, and waited a long moment. Finally, he answered.

"All right. In another minute, everyone outside will have dropped their weapons. All of them."

"How can we be guaranteed of that?" the man asked.

"I guess you're just going to have to trust me on that one, aren't you?"

Char waved for everyone to set their guns down. Grumbling, the men did as they were told. Makara seemed the least happy of all to do it.

Nothing happened for a long while. It was hard to tell whether they had accepted or not.

"Are the weapons on the ground?" the man asked.

Char grunted. "Yeah."

The shutters of the window upstairs slammed open. Inside was a man with a rifle, aiming right for Char.

"Get down!" Makara yelled.

But no shot came. Instead, the man screamed. Inside the window stood Anna, her blade slicing toward the man's neck. It cut through, severing the man's head from his body.

Anna turned quickly, slashing her sword. Another man cried out. She raised the blade above her head, and stabbed downward.

And like that, it was over. Anna wiped off her blade before sheathing it. She came to the window and looked down. "They're all dead."

Makara stood silent. It was hard to tell if she was relieved, or angry. Maybe she was both.

"I didn't even see her leave!" I said.

"That was the point," Char said. "Neither did those scumbags up there."

Makara didn't waste any more time. She ran into the building and I followed her in. The wooden interior was dark, and crowded with round circular tables. The room was narrow, but long. The bar itself sat on the right-hand side.

Two pairs of feet pounded down the steps. Anna was the first to appear. She passed us and walked outside without a word. The second was Lisa. She was tall, slender, and had long wavy brown hair and blue eyes.

Makara ran forward and embraced her. "Lisa..."

Lisa returned the gesture. "God, why did it take a hostage situation for you to come down and visit me?"

Makara pulled back. "I'm sorry. It's been so busy, with my brother being shot. I guess you've heard about that by now."

Lisa nodded. "Yeah. That's some luck. But it's good you found him." Lisa's eyes turned on me. "Who's this?"

"This is Alex," Makara said. "He's from Bunker 108, out San Bernardino way."

"Long way," Lisa said. "You've been taking care of Makara?"

"More of the opposite."

Lisa eyed me up and down. "Yeah, I believe it."

"Hey," Makara said. "He's come a long way in the week he's been out. Holding up better than I expected him to."

Lisa didn't say anything: instead she stepped behind the bar. She picked up a dirty mug and began to wipe it clean.

"Least I can do for you guys is offer you a beer," she said. "Franco makes a good ale, and he delivered a cask of it last night."

"I'm good, thanks," I said.

Makara, however, pulled up to the bar, taking a stool. She then turned to me. "I want to catch up with Lisa. Go check on Samuel?"

"Sure."

I walked out of the Bounty. I found Anna standing outside, talking to Char. When she saw me, she broke from him.

"Heading back?" she asked.

"Yeah."

"Mind if I join you?"

"Not at all."

We walked back together. I wondered why she was taking a sudden interest in me. It didn't seem like I had much to offer.

It was quiet for a long while, so I felt like I had to say something.

"How'd you get in there, anyway?"

Anna shrugged. "I have my ways."

"Are you a ninja or something?"

"Are you just asking that because I have a katana?"

"Pretty much."

"That's understandable, I guess. Most people prefer to use guns, but I think there's a lot to be said for mastering the blade. I'll use a gun, if I have to, but I can't ever bring myself to waste a bullet."

We were approaching the compound gates.

"Look," Anna said, "I heard about what happened...at Bunker 108. Losing everyone is tough, but it's a common story with a lot of people. Anyone with a surviving family member I consider lucky."

"You sound like you're speaking from experience."

"Experience is the only thing honest people can speak from." She paused. "Look, I've got to get going. Take it easy, Alex."

She turned and walked toward the front doors, and I watched her go. What she'd said resonated with me. Even if Makara didn't like her, I felt like there was the potential for a connection. It was too bad that we'd be leaving soon. Besides, I couldn't see what Anna would want with me, anyway.

I turned from the courtyard and made my way to the clinic. It was time to report to Samuel.

SIX

Samuel looked even better than he had a few hours ago. He sat up in bed and fed himself some more of the leftover stew, balancing the bowl on his knee.

"Good to see you up," I said.

Samuel grunted. "Me, too. One of the Raiders came in and told me what happened. Is everyone okay?"

"Yeah. Anna saved the day. She snuck into the building and assassinated the two guys holding Lisa hostage."

"And Lisa?"

"She's fine," I said. "She and Makara are catching up now."

Samuel shrugged and took another bite of stew.

"Char talked about the Great Blight," I said. "What is it?"

Samuel thought for a moment. "The Great Blight is the biggest obstacle we face before reaching Bunker One. Hundreds of miles of old-growth Blight. Basically, the monsters in the Great Blight will make Kari look like someone's lost pet."

It was hard to imagine any monster getting bigger

than Kari. That giant had been at least three times the size of a normal human, but at least we had escaped her.

"Char mentioned something called crawlers, too, and from the way he described them, I'm thinking we need to come up with an alternate route."

"That's the way we have to go," Samuel said. "The Great Blight stretches too far, and the shortest path will be a direct line. We'll just have to hope the Recon is faster than anything we run across. We have the turret and thousands of rounds of ammunition, in case it comes to that." He nodded. "It probably will."

"What about you? You feeling all right?"

"I feel like hell," Samuel said. "But I'll manage. I've been doing some prelim scouting."

Samuel reached for his bedside table and picked up a tattered, folded piece of paper. He unfolded it, revealing a map of the United States, along with its cities and highways. Several points on the map had been marked already – mostly in the Mojave area. A thick, red line had been drawn from Raider Bluff to Cheyenne Mountain, Colorado.

"I've been considering the most efficient route to Bunker One," Samuel said. "We'll be taking I-40 east most of the way. As we travel further east, it will get drier and drier. Our first obstacle will be a giant desert called the Boundless...nearly two hundred miles of cold desert, mesas, and dunes. Most who try to traverse it aren't heard from again. Then again, most don't have a Recon at their disposal. There will be a lot of empty, uninhabited land, but as long as we stick to the line of the old highway, we'll have a fighting chance. We'll take plenty of food and water, both for drinking and to produce hydrogen."

"And the Great Blight?"

"Honestly, I don't know what to expect. Everything is up in the air once we make the border. No one even knows where it begins, exactly. All the same, we have to go through it, all the way to Cheyenne."

"And come out again."

Samuel nodded at that, but said nothing. "It's what we have to do. Who knows? Maybe it won't be as bad as everyone says."

For some reason, I doubted that, but kept that thought to myself.

I thought of the Blight that Makara and I went through while trying to find the entrance to Bunker 114. It was hard to imagine hundreds of miles of it.

"Somewhere in there is the city of Albuquerque," Samuel said. "There, the road turns north. We'll be taking I-25 the rest of the way to Cheyenne Mountain. After that, it gets a bit trickier. We'll have to find the right roads to make it to Bunker One. If we're lucky, we'll find some signs pointing the way. If not, we always have a compass to go by."

"How long should all this take?"

Samuel shrugged. "In the Old World, two days at most. Now, who knows? It could take anywhere from a week to a month, depending on what trouble we run into."

Anna charged into the room, out of breath.

"What's going on?" I asked.

"You won't believe this, but it isn't over."

"What isn't?" Samuel asked.

"There were a group of Imperials camped to the south. Apparently, they'd come with Rex and had stayed hidden. They're torching the farms."

"The farms?" I asked.

"Char wants everyone at the front gates, stat. You included, Alex. We can't let any of them escape Bluff alive."

My heart pounded. Here I was, not even a Raider, about to go fight in their war.

"Come on!" Anna said. "He wants us at the bottom of Bluff in ten."

Anna shot out the door. I looked at Samuel.

"Don't get yourself killed. Stay with Anna and don't take any risks. Makara should be down there, too, so find her and tell her the same. Our mission is greater."

I nodded. "I know that. I'll find a nice rock to hide behind."

"Good boy."

When I walked out of the room, I caught up with Anna, who was already running for the front doors. By the time we exited to the courtyard, she spoke.

"You're a Raider now," she said. "So you better fight like one."

"I'm no Raider," I said.

She eyed my Beretta. "Hope you know how to use that."

"Well enough to have killed my share of monsters."

Anna raised an eyebrow at that. "Well, you'll be killing men today. The gate's only a couple miles down the road. I suggest we run faster."

As Anna took off, I shook my head.

"Great," I said. "I love running."

By the time we made it to the gates I was, unsurprisingly, out of breath. The fact that we went downhill the whole way worked in my favor, but still, two miles in fifteen minutes had taken its toll. We had gone down countless switchbacks to get to the desert below. The whole time, smoke poured into the sky from the fires consuming the farms. There was still time to save the greater part of the crop, but a lot of damage had already been dealt.

At the bottom of the bluff, Anna and I ran to join a

group of about twelve Raiders. Among them were Char, Makara, and Lisa. Lisa held a sniper rifle, complete with scope, in both hands, and wore a grim expression to match.

"Good, Anna's here," Char said. "Here's the full situation. There are five or six Imperials trying to escape along the river. We outnumber them two to one, but there are still enough to do damage. It's likely they'll take cover and fire on us as we approach. You know the drill, so don't do anything stupid. They've already killed several of the slaves who weren't quick enough." Char looked around at everyone. I wondered what "the drill" was, but was too afraid to ask. "Keep low, form a half-circle and flank them in. None of these Imperials need to make it home. Right, let's go!"

Char turned and charged for the river, and everyone followed.

I ran beside Makara, still wheezing from my descent.

"Samuel told me to tell you not to die."

"I won't. Stick by me and we'll be fine."

We ran for at least another mile across the rocky ground. As we got closer to the action, I could smell acrid smoke in the cold, dry air.

We arrived at a small incline, which we ran up. Cresting the rise, we caught sight of the Imperials, who were lying on the ground in wait.

"Down!" Char roared.

Their guns went off, and a couple of Raiders dropped immediately. Makara and I fell to the ground, making sure to remain hidden below the ridge line.

"Just wait here," Makara said. "We can't charge them or we'll get killed."

Every Raider was planted on the safe side of the ridge. The gunfire had faded, leaving only the wind and the sand. Sand hit my face, collected on the windward side of my body.

And then...

Crack.

It was a single, distant shot reverberating through the desert. I couldn't tell where it had come from.

Then, I heard screams. At first, I thought they were on our side, and it took me a moment to realize they were coming from the river.

Crack.

Another shot. More cries of panic.

Makara was looking toward the other Raiders. They were all lying in place, as before.

Char raised an arm. Silently, all the Raiders stood, then charged down the ridge.

I rushed to join them. Two dead Imperials lay at the bottom of the hill while the remaining three were running for the cold Colorado River.

The Raiders fired their guns, yelling, surrounding the Imperials on three sides. The Imperials ran into the water and started swimming, but two went down immediately, their bodies floating downstream. The last made a dive, vanishing below the surface of the dark blue water. We waited for a good thirty seconds before he came back up. When he did, he appeared distant, about a quarter of the way across the river.

The Raiders took aim again, but before any could take a shot, another crack sounded. The man stopped swimming, and floated downstream like the rest.

All of the Raiders gazed northward along the rise. At a high point, a figure stood with a long rifle held aloft.

Of course. Lisa had sniped them all out.

After she joined the rest of the group, we headed back to Bluff. Though the Imperials were all dead, that didn't stop the fires they'd set from burning.

SEVEN

We spent the rest of the day putting out what fires we could. Not just us, but every person that could be spared in Raider Bluff, slave or free. We worked hour after hour, throwing water gathered from the irrigation canals and river onto the stubborn flames. Often, it felt as if we were making no progress. We could do nothing for the larger fires, except ignore them.

Finally, the last of the fires had burned out, leaving a good third of Raider Bluff's farmland a smoking ruin.

The farms were just the beginning, though, because it was only a matter of time until the Empire came back. Next time, it would be more than six men. I wondered if Char was having any regrets about killing Rex.

That evening, we stood together in the clinic, Samuel having called this meeting to make an announcement. Makara had brought Lisa with her, and Char was there as well, along with Anna.

"I've brought you all here to tell you that we can't stay in Raider Bluff any longer," Samuel said. "We're leaving tomorrow."

All of us exchanged glances, not quite sure how to

react to the news. I couldn't see how he could be serious. He'd been shot in the arm just *yesterday*.

It was a while before anyone spoke.

"Absolutely not," Makara said. "You need more time to recover."

"I'll have to recover on the road," Samuel said. "This attack has convinced me. I will not be caught in Raider Bluff during a war. Moreover, Bunker One will be buried in snow if we wait that long. Even now, we're pushing it."

Makara opened her mouth, but Char held a hand up.

"Listen here," Char said. "I know you're a tough guy, but this is crazy. You leave now, that wound will open up and get infected. You want to go through the Great Blight with an open wound like that? The Empire will be back, yes. But not tomorrow. Not even in a month."

"I'll do what I must to get those Black Files," Samuel said. "Even at the risk of my own life."

"Yes," Char said, "but does Makara feel the same way?"

From the look in Makara's eyes, it was clear that she didn't. She took a step forward. "Samuel, you're not thinking straight. Like Char said, the Empire won't be here for months, and…"

"I know it's crazy," he said, "but this mission is *happening,* and it is happening *tomorrow.* The longer we stay here, the more things will fall apart. The Empire attacked Raider Bluff today, and who's to say they don't have an army camped a day's march away?" He looked at each of us in turn. His brown eyes were fierce and determined. "No, it must be tomorrow or it might never be at all. As soon as we can get outfitted, we're out of here. As for my arm, it's a risk we'll have to take, because I don't have to remind you that we're not just risking my life here. We're risking the fate of the world."

From the lack of surprise on Anna's face, I could tell that Char must have already told her about our mission. Makara noticed that, too, and didn't seem too pleased.

Everyone was quiet as we thought about this turn of events. Samuel was our leader; wherever he decided to go, I would follow. I was worried about Makara, who had made a good point. Samuel was not one hundred percent. He wasn't even fifty percent.

"We'll leave tomorrow, then," Lisa said.

Everyone stared at her in shock, except for Makara. Clearly, the two had discussed this before.

"Wait," I said. "You're coming?"

"Makara and I talked it over when you left. You guys will need me out there. I'm a deadly shot, and that's a skill you could use out there in the Great Blight."

"Yeah, you're coming," Makara said. "But we can't leave tomorrow, Lisa. Sam just isn't..."

"I don't know, Makara," Lisa said, brushing a strand of hair from across her eye. "From what you told me today...maybe Samuel is right. It's a game of time at this point, and if we wait here too long, our window to strike closes. We must move quickly if we are to succeed."

Makara scowled, but said nothing. She had been hoping for Lisa to back her, not agree with Samuel.

"As long as I don't stress my arm, I should be fine," Samuel said.

"Stress is guaranteed to happen," Makara said. "If you die on us..."

"We all have more than a chance of dying out there, Makara. I'm not easy to kill, and my determination to reach Bunker One is greater than anyone else's in this group. I think I'm the best judge of knowing whether or not I can make it."

Makara sighed, clearly unhappy. "I'm not going to

win this one, am I?" She looked at me. "What about you?"

"I think we should go," I said. "Samuel is right." I looked at Lisa. "And I'm glad to have you with us, Lisa."

She nodded in reply, but said nothing.

"I guess that's it, then," Makara said. "We're just going to let you get killed. I just hope those Files are worth the price."

"They are," Samuel said. "What's one life compared to the world? I'm not going to die, though. You'll see."

Makara didn't look too convinced about that.

"Are you sure about this?" Samuel asked, looking at Lisa. "There's a good chance we won't be coming back. Saying that our mission is dangerous would be an understatement. Don't get me wrong; we could use someone with your skills, but if you want to back out..."

"Samuel, don't insult me," Lisa said. "I'm a grown woman capable of making my own decisions. I want to help." She cracked a smile. "Besides, I've been in this town too long. I've already made arrangements for the Bounty to be run by my friend, Franco. I told him if I'm not back in three months, it's his."

"That's...very generous," Samuel said.

"I'm serious about this," Lisa said. "Makara asked me to raid with her last season, and I turned her down." She nodded. "I've been regretting that decision ever since."

"It's okay," Makara said. "It wasn't your place to go."

"All the same...I'm here, locked and loaded. The minute Makara told me about what you guys were doing, I told her I was in. I've been cooped up in that bar too long."

"We have a mission to accomplish," Samuel said.

"As long as you know how serious this is, we'll all get along fine."

"I've been nothing but serious my whole life," Lisa said, her blue eyes determined. "I'm ready."

Samuel's and Lisa's eyes met and locked for a moment. I could tell that Samuel was impressed. Turning away, he cleared his throat.

"Anyway, we're heading out tomorrow, before sunrise. I want to make it at least to the Boundless by tomorrow night, which shouldn't be a problem."

"Great," Lisa said. "I'll get my stuff ready."

Char shook his head. Up until now, he, along with Anna, had been quiet, listening to the entire exchange. Now, Char looked ready to speak his mind.

"I don't like it," he said, his voice almost a growl, "but far be it from me to stop you. You made some good points, Samuel, but it is in my medical opinion that you should give the wound another week to heal. Another week and the chance of infection goes way down. You're asking for trouble if you head out tomorrow."

Samuel listened. I could tell that Char's words carried a lot of weight, but Samuel remained resolute. "No. It's now or never. I feel it in my bones."

Char nodded. "So be it. Feelings like that rarely lie."

I wondered what was going through Anna's mind. I had the crazy thought that she might come with us, only she needed to stay and protect Char. Besides, she and Makara had gotten off on the wrong foot. I didn't relish the thought of them picking at each other the entire way. Still, part of me wished she could come.

"If there is anything you can't find in the stores," Char said, "come see me and I'll supply it myself."

With a nod, Char left the room. Anna followed, giving one last glance. Her eyes found mine before she disappeared into the corridor.

"I've already mapped our journey," Samuel said. "I

don't know how long it will take, but I expect plenty of roadblocks along the way, especially once we make it to the Great Blight. You guys can spend the rest of the evening figuring out what we need. Alex has all the batts to buy supplies – we just need plenty of cold weather gear, as well as ammunition...pretty much replacements for everything we lost in Bunker 114. Makara, you're good at that kind of thing, so you're in charge. Take the batts and make sure we're stocked for the journey."

"Lisa and I will take care of it," she said.

"What can I do?" I asked.

"Get the Recon prepped. Ask around for the garage head and have them take a look at it. The last thing we need is for it to break down from something we could have prevented here. Securing extra water would also be good. Get the largest containers you can and load them on."

"I can have Franco bring some empty casks up from the Bounty," Lisa said. "There's at least twenty in the basements."

"That's perfect," Samuel said. "Fit as much as you can into the cargo bay. Once you're done, help out where you can."

"Sounds good," I said.

"Take care out there," Samuel said. "I wish I could help you, but..."

"You stay here," Makara said. "We'll take care of everything."

That was it, then. Tomorrow, we left for Bunker One.

THE NEXT MORNING HADN'T EVEN DAWNED, BUT WE ALL stood in the courtyard in the dry cold, making last minute preparations on the Recon. I stood bleary-eyed, grumpy, cold, and hungry, every bone and muscle aching in my body. I had spent half the night making sure the Recon was prepped, as well as helping Makara and Lisa pack everything up. After that, we triple-checked that we had everything we needed.

After asking around a bit, I had found a man named Tony, who was the garage head for the compound. He ran a diagnostic and I was relieved to hear the Recon had no issues that he could see. The Recon was a bit beyond his scope, so if anything, he was glad to get a chance to check it out. Tony made recommendations for spare parts and once Makara returned from shopping, he showed us how to replace those parts in case they broke down.

Besides the Recon, we had food stocked for a month, two hundred and fifty gallons of water (mostly for refu-eling), cold weather gear including snow boots and parkas, face masks, medicine, bandages, cooking equip-ment, a few extra rifles, and plenty of ammunition. We had spent every last batt to get all of these things, along with dipping into Makara's own credit from past raids.

And now, it looked as if we were finally ready to set off. I looked for Anna among the small group of Raiders that had gathered, but I was disappointed to see she wasn't there.

Char stood before Makara. At first, they grabbed each other's forearms with both hands – a typical Raider gesture, I guess. Char then hugged Makara tightly.

"Be safe out there, kid," he said. "Come back in one piece."

"I'll try, Char."

Char pulled back, and with that, we got in the Recon. Makara settled behind the wheel while Samuel took the passenger's seat. Lisa checked to make sure the cargo bay was secure before she climbed in, putting in her long sniper rifle first. I was the last inside, and no sooner had I strapped myself in did Makara turn the key in the ignition.

The engine roared to life and the needle on the dash climbed as pressure built in the hydrogen tank. The wheels moved, and we drove toward the open gates of the compound.

No one said anything as we navigated the city's dirt roads. In a matter of weeks, maybe days, we would be in Bunker One – assuming we didn't die before that. I couldn't think about that, though. Not now.

We had brought antibiotics in case Samuel's wound acted up. So far he had given no signs of distress. I didn't know if it was because he was truly okay, or if he was just hiding the pain. Probably the second one. His left arm would be in a sling for a while, but his right hand could still aim and shoot.

We were on the bottom level of Bluff. At this early hour, the streets were completely empty. We made a final turn before approaching the open gates.

"Oh no," Makara said.

"What?" I asked.

She merely stared ahead, where a figure stood, shadowed in the predawn.

"It's...*her!*"

Makara was right. It was Anna, standing in front of the city gates with her katana drawn.

EIGHT

Makara stepped on the accelerator.

"Makara, what are you doing?" I asked.

"She is *not* coming with us."

"Well, she definitely won't if you *kill* her!"

"Makara, stop!" Samuel said.

The words went unheeded. Anna stood her ground, staring defiantly at the oncoming Recon. Makara was not slowing down. In fact, she only went faster.

"Well," Lisa said, "this has gotten interesting really fast."

At the last moment, when it looked as if Anna was going to get run over, Makara slammed on the brakes. Still, Anna stood her ground.

The vehicle skidded to the right, nearing the cliff edge. Finally, at the last possible moment, Anna jumped out of the way.

Makara regained control, flooring it. The gates of Raider Bluff were left behind as we sped down the narrow road, narrowly missing falling off the cliff.

"Slow down, Makara!" Samuel said. "You're going to kill us all!"

"She thought she could stop us," Makara said. "I guess I proved her wrong."

"Makara...enough." Samuel said. "This is insane."

"It doesn't matter," she said, relaxing. "It's done."

Lisa chuckled. "You've always liked the more direct approach."

It was hard to decide who was the craziest – Makara, who had tried to run over Anna, or Anna, who stood her ground so long, or Lisa, who just found the whole thing funny.

"You really don't like her, huh?" I asked.

My question went unanswered when I heard the roar of an engine behind us. I looked in the side mirror, seeing that a single headlight had materialized in the predawn darkness.

Clearly, it wasn't over yet.

"She's following us!" Makara said.

She flipped on the LCD screen in the center of the dashboard, which revealed the dirt road behind us and the single headlight growing larger and brighter. The shape of a motorcycle appeared, along with the shadowy form of Anna, her black hair blowing in the wind.

"When we get to the bottom, I'm gunning it," Makara said. "We'll leave her in our dust."

"Makara, just stop the car," I said. "There's no way we can outrun her. She might have something important to say."

"She wants to come with us," Makara said, "and I'm not having it."

"I don't get it," I said. "She'd be useful. You saw what she did with that blade."

We snaked back and forth down the mesa. When we reached the bottom, Makara sped up, heading due east toward a brightening crimson sky. Anna only matched our pace. That motorcycle could go faster than us, easily, but if Makara was anything, it was stubborn. She pressed the accelerator until the Recon's engine was roaring, until the hydrogen fuel tank gave a miserable high whine. The pressure needle climbed and climbed, into the red.

She was going to make the thing explode.

"Makara, pull over!" Samuel said.

"No."

"Pull over, goddamn it! She's coming with us whether you like it or not!"

Makara slammed on the brakes, causing us all to rock forward in our seats. The seatbelt pressed into my neck, constricting my breathing. On the LCD screen, the headlight grew brighter and brighter.

I saw what Makara had intended all along; Anna was going to crash into us.

But instead, Anna veered off, flashing past the Recon's right side mere inches away. She circled around to the Recon's driver's side and halted, cutting off the engine. Her face was calm and implacable. To her, a couple of brushes with death in five minutes' time were all in a day's work.

Samuel and I got out of the Recon, but Makara and Lisa stayed inside.

Outside, the air was sharp and dry. The sun had lit the land dull red from behind equally red clouds. Mountains towered in the distance to the east, and the desert of rock and sand stretched flat to meet them. Behind us, Raider Bluff sat on its cliff, dark and brooding in the early hour.

"I'm coming with you," Anna said simply.

"Did Char send you?" Samuel asked. "Makara will give me hell if I let you into the Recon."

"No, Char didn't send me. That's why I met you at the gate. He wouldn't have wanted me to come. You guys need me, though, as a guide. The terrain is dangerous, and I'm the only one in Bluff who can lead you to the Great Blight."

"What makes you think that we can't make it on our own?"

Anna shrugged. "Maybe you can. But I know the Boundless. My mother and I wandered there, for a while, before I found my way here. I can at least lead you straight to the border without you running into any of the Desert Tribes."

"No one can guarantee that," Samuel said. "They're nomadic."

"Well," Anna said, "your chances will be better with me leading the way. My bike can be stored in the cargo bay until it's time for me to go. It's capable of high mileage, so getting home shouldn't be an issue, even if I can't find water."

At that moment, Makara jumped from the Recon and walked up to Anna. Lisa rolled down the window to listen, intently interested.

"You are *not* coming."

"You would be wrong, then. Last I checked, you weren't the leader of this expedition."

Makara's eyes cut dangerously at Anna. It looked as if things were going to come to blows.

"I don't want you here," Makara said. "End of story."

Makara's hand made its way to her holstered handgun. The movement didn't escape Anna's attention, whose hand moved to the hilt of her blade.

"Stop this madness," Samuel said.

"We don't *need* her help," Makara said.

Anna stepped forward, her eyes challenging. "You don't? Spoken like someone who has never seen the Boundless. Do you know where the Desert Tribes camp? Do you know which mesas are safe to hide behind in a dust storm?"

From Makara's silence, it seemed as if she didn't know the answers to either of those questions.

"You're leaving once we get to the Great Blight, then?"

"That's the plan."

"What's in this for you?"

"Char told me about your mission," Anna said. "I just want to do my bit to help. I'll be out of your hair in a couple of days. That much I promise."

Makara sighed, realizing that was the best deal she could get. "Fine. But if you're not gone by the time we get to the Great Blight, I'll make *sure* you're gone. Whether that's you riding off into the sunset, or riding into the next life with a bullet in your head, I'll see it done." She paused. "Am I clear on that?"

Anna appeared completely nonplussed. Turning on her heel, Makara went back into the Recon.

"Don't say anything to incite Makara," Samuel said to Anna. "If you're going to be with us for the next few days, I want this trip to be as peaceful as possible."

Anna nodded. "I know this is last-minute, but I really believe you guys will need my help. After the Great Blight, you'll be on your own."

"We need to get moving," Samuel said. "We can't get bogged down on who doesn't like whom. We have a mission to finish."

Once the motorcycle was stowed in the cargo bay, we piled into the Recon and continued our journey. Anna took my seat by the window while I sat in the middle between her and Lisa. I figured Lisa would side with Makara out of loyalty, so I just wanted to keep things as calm as possible.

The silence in the cab was tense, and the way was bumpy. In time, I began to nod off a bit. When I woke from my doze, the day brightened, the crimson Wasteland passed at a solid clip. It was amazing how fast the Recon could go.

"We should be there in a few days, right?" I said.

"Now is the easy part," Makara said. "The road gets much tougher further ahead."

As the day wore on, large dunes replaced the flat and rocky ground. It was difficult to pick our way past them. Anna pointed the way, but I couldn't see how she discerned one dune from the other. Makara took Anna's directions grudgingly, but even she wasn't going to ignore her expertise.

By midday, our progress had slowed to a near stand-still. We were doing fifteen miles an hour over the dunes, where an hour ago we had been doing fifty.

"We made it to the Boundless," Anna said. "No trick here, just keep heading east."

"If the engine doesn't clog with sand," Makara said.

After we slogged through the dunes a couple more hours, I saw a long jagged line in the distance.

"What's that?" I asked.

"Looks like a canyon," Makara said. "Does it head the right way?"

Anna didn't answer for a bit. "I think so."

"I need more than that, expert," Makara said, with biting sarcasm. "Are we going in, or what?"

Anna hesitated a moment. "I'm sure this canyon heads east. We left the highway south, but that would just be a lot of backtracking."

"You don't sound so sure."

I spoke up. "I don't know if it's from some book or a movie I saw, but I think going in there is a really bad idea..."

At last, Anna spoke. "Do it."

"You got it," Makara said.

She headed straight for the canyon, and a few minutes later, we had entered its gaping entrance. As we drove deeper within, the jagged brown rock on either side rose higher and higher. Anna seemed to be correct; it more or less headed east, but there was no telling whether there was an exit at the end. It zigzagged back and forth, making it difficult to see too far ahead. We were doing forty miles an hour, much better than our earlier progress, but whether that stayed the same remained to be seen.

Finally, we made a turn, entering a long, wide stretch where sheer cliff rose up on either side.

And that was when a bullet cracked the Recon's windshield.

NINE

A long the right-hand rim of the canyon, men appeared, aiming rifles down at the Recon. Bullets dinged off the vehicle's sides and cracked the wind-shield further.

"Damn it!" she said. "I thought you said we wouldn't be running into the Desert Tribes!"

Before Anna could respond, a bullet hit where it shouldn't have – one of the back tires. There was a pop as the thick rubber was reduced to uselessness, grinding the Recon to a halt. Before the vehicle had completely stopped, Makara spun the wheel and faced the vehicle sideways toward our attackers. As everyone ducked, more bullets riddled the Recon's side.

"Get out the other side!" Samuel said. "We'll use the Recon for cover."

We rushed to get out as yet more bullets ripped into the Recon's side. I tumbled into the dirt, seeing that the opposite side of the canyon was clear. Beside me, Lisa emerged, kneeling on the ground and snapping a scope onto her rifle. Once done, she put it to her eye, scanning the empty rim of the canyon for threats.

"This side looks clear," she said.

Anna peered through the Recon's windows to the other side. "Looks like some of them are trying to find another angle."

"Who the hell are these people?" Makara asked Anna. "Why did you lead us here?"

"Stop fighting," Samuel said. "It isn't helping. We need to figure out how to take these guys down. In the meantime, we can get to work on the tire."

At the top of the canyon, a man showed himself from behind a rock, aiming his rifle down. My ears nearly split when Lisa's sniper rifle fired. It was a direct hit; the man screamed as he fell forward into the canyon.

Makara looked at the mangled tire doubtfully. "The jack and the spare are both in the cargo bay. If we go in through the back we'll be exposed."

"So how do we get that tire out?" I asked. "It won't fit through the cab."

Everyone thought for a moment. Thinking, however, was a difficult thing to do under enemy fire.

"Maybe Lisa can snipe them all out," I said.

"That won't work," she said. "By the time I set up a position they will have sniped *me* out."

"Not if you're inside the Recon, with the window cracked just enough to aim your gun out. The glass is bulletproof. As long as you can see through the glass with your scope, you should be able to fire safely. That might give the rest of us the cover we need to get the tire."

"That...might actually work."

"Get to it, then." Samuel said. "And be careful."

"You might want to cover your ears," Lisa said.

Lisa jumped back into the Recon, taking up a position behind the second window. She quickly put in ear plugs. A few more bullets were fired from the rim of the canyon as Lisa lowered the window, ever so slightly, until she could stick the barrel out.

"This is more than a little awkward."

"Just do your best," Samuel said. "This is all we've got."

Lisa let out a breath and paused a moment before the loud crack of the rifle echoed off the rock walls. She fired again, again, and again...

The bullets from above stopped raining down.

"They've taken cover," Lisa shouted. "Now's your chance."

Makara and I ran around the side of the vehicle, only to have a bullet ricochet off the ground at our feet. We opened the door, hopping into the cargo bay before any more bullets could be fired at us. The tire was mounted on the wall on the right side. We grabbed the tire and jack and carried both back to the group.

"Let Makara work," Samuel said. "You stand guard."

From time to time, Lisa's sniper rifle fired, sending a deafening blast throughout the canyon. Anna stood nearby with her pistol out, scanning the rim of the canyon above.

The Recon had already been lifted from the ground. Makara had the mangled tire off in less than a minute.

"Brings back old times in L.A.," Samuel said.

"They're running away," Lisa said, withdrawing from the Recon.

"A diversion?" Anna asked.

Makara was now lowering the jack. The new tire was on, and we were ready to resume our journey.

"All done," she said. "Get back in so we can..."

But she was interrupted when an otherworldly bellow permeated the canyon.

"What the *hell* was that?" Lisa asked.

Everything seemed to go quiet, until a giant creature

appeared from around the corner of the canyon we had come from. It was humanoid, like Kari, but unlike Kari, it was at least twice as big. It snarled as it spied us, and bounded toward us on thick legs.

"In the Recon, *now!*" Samuel yelled.

We rushed to get inside. Makara turned the key in the ignition. The ground shook with each of the creature's steps.

"What is it?" I asked, once inside.

"Just go!" Samuel said.

As the Recon tore through the dirt, Makara clicked on the LCD, revealing the giant creature giving chase. It was at least twenty feet tall, with thick muscles that only made it bigger. Like Kari, the skin looked stretched, evidenced by the rips through which purple pus oozed. Its eyes shone brightly, completely white.

It seemed to keep pace with the vehicle.

"Alex, do something!" Makara yelled.

"Against *that?*"

"Get to the turret! *Now!*"

The Recon surged ahead as the creature's extended claws scratched the back of the vehicle. We gained a bit of distance from the push, but the respite wasn't to last. The creature closed the gap, nearing the Recon once again.

I got up and ran to the back, climbing the short ladder to the turret. I opened the hatch and stepped through, trying not to let the bumps and sharp turns throw me off balance. The giant machine gun was waiting for me.

It was pointing ahead, so I wheeled it around until it was facing the giant beast. It was closer than ever, just a few strides away, and I had to point the gun upward just to aim at its head. Its grotesque mouth was agape, revealing rows of razor-sharp yellow teeth, its white eyes burning fiercely. Upon seeing me, it gave a roar and charged forward.

I squeezed the trigger. Nothing happened.

The monster reached an arm back, its eyes igniting in bloodlust.

Anna emerged from the bay below.

"Anna!"

She reached for something on the gun. "Try turning the safety off next time."

A moment later, a hail of bullets streamed from the end of the gun, splattering the legs and abdomen of the monster. It bellowed in pain, but it seemed I had only succeeded in pissing it off and making it charge faster.

"Aim for the eyes!" Anna shouted.

I swiveled the weapon upward, holding it steady. I let the monster have it again, and this time, the bullets entered its neck and face. It gave a horrible wail, falling to its knees. I kept shooting. Somehow, I was able to train the gun on its face, and more bullets entered its head. The thing fell into the dirt and went still.

Anna grabbed my arm, making me release pressure from the trigger.

"It's dead," she said.

Indeed it was. The thing was slumped on the ground, purple, sticky liquid gushing from the holes I'd made in its face.

We stood there a moment as the Recon kept driving, the cold wind chilling my face. My hands were still glued to the gun.

Anna put her hands on mine, and one by one released each of my fingers from the grips. She let go, remembering herself, before looking at me.

"You okay?"

"Yeah," I said. "I think so."

We stood there for another moment, watching as the

monster disappeared from view as the Recon rounded another bend.

"What *was* that?"

"I've never seen one myself," Anna said, "but I've heard people tell stories about them. Until today, I didn't believe they were real." She paused. "They're called Behemoths."

"This would be the second I killed."

Anna looked at me, a newfound respect in her eyes. "Let's hope it's the last. We should get inside."

After I clicked the safety back on, we reentered the cargo bay and closed the hatch above us.

By the time we got back to the cab, everyone was ecstatic.

"Good job," Samuel said. "Couldn't have done it better myself."

"Yeah," Makara said. "It should be clear sailing from here."

"Good work, Alex," Lisa said.

"It was nothing," I said. "Without Anna, it might've gone differently."

"This one is yours," Anna said. "If this is just the first day, I'm sure I'll have plenty of other chances."

That made everyone go quiet. In a short time, the canyon became shallower, and soon, we had reemerged into the arid Boundless. Hundreds of red dunes spread in all directions, stopped only by lines of jagged mountains far to the east. It would be hell trying to get through those. It was late afternoon, and the light was already failing.

But the dunes were not what worried me most. In the distance to the east was a low, menacing wall of cloud tumbling toward us. I remembered the Devil's Wall Makara and I had weathered back in the Mojave.

"Dust storm," Lisa said. "And nowhere to hide."

"Where do we wait it out?" I asked.

Samuel pointed toward the left. "Let's head to that mesa. It's maybe a klick out."

"Do it," Anna said. "If we stay on the mesa's leeward side, we should be safe."

Makara was going full speed, racing against the clouds advancing toward us. The swirling wall of dust and flashing lightning expanded ever outward with malevolence, as if it existed only to harm us. Thundering and crashing with Jovian force, it could bury the entire Recon in quick order, rendering it useless, or worse, rendering us dead.

One by one, the dunes in the distance were lost as the wall overtook them. We were closer to the mesa. The only thing was, I didn't know if we were close enough.

Finally the dunes ended, and a large flatland separated us from the mesa. The dust was on our right, just seconds away.

"We're not going to make it," Lisa said.

"Hold on tight," Makara said.

The Recon's headlights clicked on. The land before us was eerily calm and quiet. On our right was the thrashing maelstrom.

With the force of a colossal hammer, the wind slammed into us, nearly upturning the Recon vehicle. It spun us toward the south, forcing us to follow that direction.

"We have to make it to the mesa," Samuel said. "That wind will make us crash into something."

"Almost there," Makara said.

I couldn't see anything out the windshield, so I knew Makara couldn't, either. She kept the compass on the dash pointed northeast – the direction we had been going earlier to hit the mesa. The wind pummeled the side of the Recon and lightning crackled around us.

That was the worst part – the lightning. I tried not to picture myself getting fried to a crisp.

The wind died as we reached the mesa. Makara slammed on the brakes. We slowed to a stop, mere feet away from having crashed into the rock.

"Well...we made it," Makara said.

"What now?" I asked.

"It's nearing nightfall, anyway," Samuel said. "It's best to just eat and sleep."

As the storm's eddies pounded into the Recon's sides, Makara hooked up the stove to the dash to get started on dinner. While it cooked, I closed my eyes in my seat, not even bothering to take off my seatbelt. The sounds of the raging storm, just inches away through the pane of glass, lulled me into a doze.

The smell of cooking stew roused me from my slumber. Outside, it was still dark, windy, and it had gotten cold inside the cab, despite the five bodies and the stove warming it.

We ate, the hearty stew doing a bit to warm me. Makara started the Recon in order to charge the battery, before shutting it off a few minutes later. Lisa made me stand, that way she could lift my seat and enter the cargo bay. She set up her roll and blanket there. It was only 2100 by now, but it seemed as if everyone was exhausted. After a minute, Makara went back to join Lisa, while Anna was already fast asleep, leaning her head against the window against which the sand buffeted.

Only Samuel and I remained awake. Samuel was looking over his map, marking our location with a red pen.

"Good progress for the first day," Samuel said, "all things considered."

"How much longer, you think?"

He shrugged. "Impossible to say from here. That will become clearer once we pass the Boundless. I don't know what the Great Blight will be like, so I'm in the dark as much as you."

"We all are, aren't we?"

Samuel nodded. "We're going where no one has ever gone. Not only that, but we have to survive it, and return alive." Samuel looked out the window, at the swirling sand. "Get some sleep, Alex. We've got a long day ahead of us tomorrow."

TEN

The storm had cleared at some point in the night, and when we woke, the tires of the Recon were buried in about a foot of sand. We easily got moving, though, and ate a cold breakfast on the road.

We had been traveling east for an hour when we noticed a cloud of dust trailing behind.

"That's not another dust storm, is it?" I asked.

"It's not a dust storm," Makara said. "It's something else."

Anna gazed out the window. "Something's moving inside it."

A sound soon accompanied the dust – the roar of engines. Within the dust cloud were about a dozen gleaming vehicles moving across the desert flatland. They were too small to be cars.

"Motorcycles," Anna said.

"Great," Makara said. "Whose turn is it to man the turret this time?"

"They might be friendlies," Anna said.

"They might not," Samuel said. "Still, we don't open fire until they shoot at us."

"What should I do, stop?" Makara asked. "They're faster."

"Is there a good position nearby?"

"No," Makara said. "It's all flat out here. There's some dunes farther east, but we won't make it in time."

We continued driving. As the minutes passed, the bikes got all the closer. The forerunner seemed to be waving a flag of some sort.

"What does it mean?" I asked.

"Either they're telling us their friendly, or they're tricking us," Makara said.

"Lisa, man the turret," Samuel said. "If they fire, you know what to do."

"On it."

I moved in my seat, allowing Lisa access to the cargo bay.

"Should we keep moving, or...?"

"Keep moving," Samuel said.

Another few minutes passed. The bikes came into range of the turret – there looked to be a dozen or so. The man waving the dust-stained flag seemed to be doing so more vigorously.

"I don't think they want to hurt us," Makara said. "Should I stop?"

Samuel's eye calculated, but he said nothing.

In time, one of the riders pulled even with Makara's window. He held up both hands for a moment, showing they weren't armed, before returning them to the handlebars. He had a square face, sunglasses, a leather jacket, and a long, red beard blowing in the wind.

"I feel like I've seen him before."

He signaled for Makara to roll down the window.

"Stop," Samuel said. "Alex...go get Lisa."

As Makara slowed the Recon, I went to the turret to tell Lisa to come back to the cab. She gave one last look to the surrounding bikers before descending the ladder and closing the hatch.

Once the Recon had come to a full stop, the bikers cut their engines. The man with the red beard motioned us to come out.

"All of you stay here," Samuel said. "I'm going out to meet them."

"You can't go alone," Makara said.

"You're needed in case things go wrong. I've made notes on my map, so you should be able to find the rest of the way on your own. I don't think it'll come to that, though. I'll let you know if it's safe."

Before anyone could protest further, Samuel stepped outside. His form was lost to the dust the bikes had kicked up. I didn't know if he was being brave or stupid.

"Stubborn," Lisa said.

Slowly, the fine dust settled back into the land, revealing Samuel talking to the red-bearded, tattooed man astride a black chopper. All the bikes were remnants of the Old World, and these had seen more miles than they were designed for. They were dusty, beaten, and definitely looked the worse for wear. Still, any sort of bike would be a prized possession in this world.

Samuel turned, signaling us to come out. I exited the Recon and stood beside Samuel. The biker looked like he was the leader, and his beard came down to his chest. His face was weathered and pockmarked, and his sunglasses were so dark that I was surprised he could even see out of them. I guessed he was probably in his late forties.

Makara, Lisa, and Anna stepped out to join us. Makara kept her hand on her handgun while Anna looked ready to draw her katana.

"Don't," the man said. "That would be very foolish."

Slowly, Makara and Anna took their hands from their weapons.

"Why did you stop us?" Samuel asked.

"Anyone who wishes to cross the Boundless must speak to us first. Who are you, and what brings you here? Are you from Raider Bluff?"

"We've come from Raider Bluff," Samuel said. "We aren't affiliated with them, though."

This caused the men to mumble, and some moved their hands closer to their guns. The leader raised a hand, and everyone waited for him to continue.

"No one leaves or enters Raider Bluff, except Raiders. Are you just saying that because you know the Raiders are our enemies?"

Samuel shook his head. "I don't know who you are, so no. We're traveling east to the Great Blight, on a mission that takes us to Colorado. I can't really say anything more than that, but we don't mean harm to you or your men, or any settlements under your control. We merely wish to pass through peacefully. We have our own supplies, so we won't be a drain on your resources."

"The Exiles have no settlements to their name," the man said. "We are mercenaries, usually hired to protect towns from the Raiders. Even now, we're in search of a Behemoth, which we've been tracking west."

"We killed a Behemoth west of here," Samuel said. "That was yesterday, so it probably wasn't the same one."

The man raised an eyebrow at that. "It may, or may not be. Where did you kill it?"

"A canyon, about two hours due west of here."

Again, the men murmured as they absorbed the news.

"If that's true, then you have saved us a lot of time. Still, we'll need to ride there to confirm the kill."

"It should still be there," Samuel said.

The man nodded, holding out his hand. "My name is Marcus...and we are the Exiles.

Samuel shook his hand, and introduced us all.

"You said you're traveling to the Great Blight?" Marcus asked.

"We have to," Samuel said. "I can't say anything more, because our mission is secret."

"I see. Commissioned by the Raiders?"

Samuel shook his head. "Commissioned by ourselves."

"You've got me curious," Marcus said. "I would laugh, except I can tell you're serious. If you're secret mission is to die, then you'll be successful."

Some of the Exiles chuckled, but Samuel wasn't affected by it.

"I realize it's dangerous," Samuel said. "Still, that's where the road leads." He paused, as if considering what to say next. "We believe there is some research in one of the Bunkers already covered with the Great Blight...research which might help us stop the Blights from spreading."

Marcus's brows knit together as he contemplated. "Which Bunker is that?"

Samuel hesitated a moment. "Bunker One."

Marcus whistled. "All right, now I *know* you're going to die. Do yourselves a favor: turn back."

"We can't do that, Marcus," Samuel said.

Makara stepped forward. "What do you have against the Raiders, anyway?"

Marcus looked at her. "Quiet, girl. Char can't help you here."

"What do you know about Char?"

Marcus chuckled. "You have no clue, do you? You think you're tough, but all I can hear is your big mouth."

Makara's face burned, but she didn't drop her gaze.

"Char is my brother. I think I'm qualified to know exactly who he is."

Makara's eyes widened. It was clear she didn't believe him at first, but I remembered what she'd said in the Recon: that Marcus looked familiar. Now, we knew the reason. He did have a striking resemblance to the Alpha of Raider Bluff.

"Char has never mentioned having a brother," Makara finally said.

"That doesn't surprise me," Marcus said. "Twelve years ago, we Exiles used to be Raiders. We split from them over a disagreement. We were much greater in number, once. Now, we are only thirty-two. Who you see here is just a portion of our number."

"What was the disagreement about?" Samuel asked.

"It was long ago, but it changed Raider Bluff forever, into what it is today. Twelve years ago the Raiders blew up Hoover Dam, causing a flood. It wiped out many settlements along the river."

"Why did they do that?" I asked.

"Raider Bluff had a rival, across the water on the Colorado's western shore," Marcus said. "It was called Rivertown. The Raiders believed blowing up the dam was the easiest way to destroy them. What they didn't foresee, however, was just how much death there would be. Char was young at the time, and brash. He was for the plan, and was chosen to lead the group that destroyed the dam. I fought to keep him from going. In my rage, I threw him into the fireplace of a bar we were both in. He landed face first."

No one said anything in the silence that followed. Char had received his burn from his own brother, no less.

"For my crime," Marcus said, "I was exiled. But I didn't go alone. My brothers here joined me, and many more have died in the last twelve years. It was our intent to cross the country and begin a new city, far from the troubles of the west. But we never made it that far. We were attacked by monsters on the Texas border. Even then, the Great Blight was all but impossible to cross. There was nothing we could do but turn back, and as soon as we did, the monsters went away. We tried again, years later, but we were stopped again. In the north, we were locked in by cold and snow; in the south, by the Empire, who promised us passage in exchange for military service." Marcus shook his head. "But they didn't keep their word."

"Raider Bluff is different, now," Makara said. "Char has changed."

"I swore a time would come in which they would need us. And I still believe that. But I am too proud to return."

"They need your help now more than ever," Makara said. "There will be war with the Empire, soon."

"Raider Bluff will lose that war. For every man they have, the Empire has a hundred. They may not be as strong, but that won't matter. All who have stood against the Empire have fallen. Their army numbers in the thousands. They control most of Mexico, and are extending their way north, year by year."

"They seemed to come out of nowhere," Makara said.

"I am old enough to remember. The people went south, when Ragnarok fell. There were stories about how it wasn't cold, like America was. Many thousands traveled south. Mexican, American, it didn't matter anymore. What few survived banded together. And what the people found, for the most part, is true. The Empire existed even before Ragnarok, though it went by a different name. The land of Nova Roma is temperate, good for crops, and their armies offered protection.

Hundreds of cities survived, on the coasts, on the rivers, in the forests. They warred and fought, their wealth fueled by slavery, guns, and bullets. When one city lost, it became the thrall of another.

"But then the Empire came, based in the city of Nova Roma. Perhaps by borrowing the empire of the same name, that existed two thousand years ago, they hoped to capture some of the magic. Their people were strong, and they subjugated their neighbors, led by a man calling himself Augustus. Instead of enslaving their neighbors, they annexed them, giving them the rights of citizenship. More people flocked to the Empire as they gained wealth and power. The Empire offered safety and law in a time of lawlessness. Within ten years, half of Mexico was theirs, and any who challenged them faced slavery or worse."

"Why are they coming here, though?" Samuel asked.

"They seek the Bunkers."

"The Bunkers?" I asked. "Why would they want them?"

"The Empire is very interested in any technology they can acquire. And not just technology, but information. There are weapons, vehicles, fuel, supplies, medicines, all of which can simply no longer be made. And it's all for the taking, whether or not it's covered by Blights. They've already raided the Bunkers closer to home, but their main prize is Bunker One...and if it weren't for the hostility of the Great Blight, they would have scrapped it long ago."

"How do you know all this?" Makara asked.

"Like I said, we Exiles wander," Marcus said. "We have on occasion hired ourselves out as mercenaries to the Novans."

The Empire's wanting to find Bunker One put them in direct competition with us. Did they know about the Black Files?

"We've already talked too much," Marcus said.

"So, we can pass your lands in peace?" Samuel asked.

Marcus nodded. "I would normally exact tribute, but I believe in the importance of your mission. The Blights have not yet touched the Empire, but they will one day, soon. Maybe the time of the Raiders is over, but at least others might be saved for a future age."

"Hopefully, everyone can be saved," Samuel said. "But only if we can make it."

"The Great Blight is dangerous beyond even what you know, Samuel," Marcus said. "You will travel upward into the mountains to the east, past the ruins of Flagstaff. It will only be another hundred miles to the border. You will not be attacked by us or anyone else on the way there. But once you cross that line, no one can help you. There are only the countless monsters that call that land their home. When you cross over, crawlers will be the least of your worries."

Marcus started his engine. The rest of the Exiles followed suit, sending a roar across the desert.

Marcus gave a salute before wheeling around, hitting full throttle as he blazed into the desert. The rest of his bikers followed him, spewing a cloud of dust that left us coughing.

When the noise faded, Samuel spoke.

"He gave us a lot to think about. The Empire worries me."

"One day at a time," Makara said. "One mission at a time."

"I suppose you're right." He turned away from the train of bikers for the Recon. "Let's move."

THAT NIGHT WE CAMPED NORTH OF THE RUINS OF Flagstaff. We went off the road a fair distance to avoid the town, since we didn't know what might be waiting there.

We found the perfect hideout – a shallow cave inside one of the rocky hills below the base of a tall mountain, the cap of which was lost in red cloud.

The landscape had changed greatly with elevation. Besides the drastic temperature drop (the thermometer in the Recon read 24° Fahrenheit), I saw my first trees – at least, the first trees that hadn't been turned by the xenovirus. They were pines mostly, and most had been long dead. What few were left alive had the barest tufts of green needles on their branches, indicating that soon they would be joining the rest.

After we stopped, we collected a lot of wood for a fire. Once we had the fire roaring, the warmth felt good.

Though the fire was warm, the night outside was bitterly cold. Anna cooked the evening meal – the same stew we had eaten last night, with the veggies, potatoes, and camel meat taken from Raider Bluff.

She came to sit near me, but we didn't speak. Everyone was watching the fire and looked exhausted. Lisa had already wrapped herself in her blanket with her back to the flame.

"Got cold, didn't it?" she asked.

"We climbed a lot in elevation," I said.

"The air does seem thinner," Anna said. "Or maybe I'm just imagining it."

We watched the fires, as one of the logs split and sent a shower of sparks upward. Makara was sharpening her knife, while Samuel, as usual, was poring over his map.

"What's your story, anyway?" I asked.

Anna shrugged. "It's not really worth telling."

"Somehow, I doubt that."

"Well, that's code for I don't really want to talk about it."

"Ouch."

"Yeah," Anna said. "I guess you could say there's a lot of ouch in it."

"I guess this is the kind of world where you can't really ask that question and expect a fairytale."

"I don't think the world ever worked like that. People like to talk about the Old World, especially the old people, like it's this magical place." Anna shook her head. "I don't believe it."

"We can see the ruins, though," I said. "They built some amazing things."

"I believe there was a world like that," Anna said. "It was only thirty years ago. Even men like Char can remember back that far. But it's amazing, really, how everything fades. How long until we believe gods made those buildings instead of men?"

I didn't know why, but the thought chilled me. "There might not even be time for that."

Anna looked at me for the first time. "Because of the xenovirus?"

I nodded. "If it's anything like what Samuel thinks it is...we probably don't have long."

Anna looked away. "That serious, then."

I nodded. "I think Samuel's right. My dad..."

Anna was listening, but I stopped myself. I didn't really want to talk about my dad.

"I should check on that stew."

She got up and lifted the lid, giving it a stir before coming to sit by me. I didn't continue talking. If Anna didn't have to tell her story, then neither did I.

A few minutes later, Anna took the pot off and started serving people. I got out my bowl and had it filled, and within minutes, it was cool enough to eat. I was halfway through my bowl, when Makara called out.

"Hey!"

The outburst made me nearly drop my bowl. I looked up to see everyone watching the mouth of the cave, where the shadowy form of a man stood.

ELEVEN

A s everyone drew their weapons, the man stepped into the firelight, revealing himself to be a stooped old man wearing a cloak and hood. He had no weapon other than his gnarled walking stick.

"Stop right there!" Samuel said. "Not a step closer."

The old man paused. By the firelight, I noticed something strange about his bright, gray eyes. They seemed to stare off, not seeing anything.

He was blind.

Everyone took in this fact at the same time just as the man started speaking.

"I felt the warmth of the fire from afar. I heard voices, and I smelled the food. I've been wandering for days, and was wondering if I might have a bite and a rest."

No one said anything, suspecting a trap. Raiders did this, sometimes – used a distraction to catch groups unaware. If only he knew about the weapons pointed at him, would he have been so calm?

"You're blind," Samuel said. "No blind man can survive alone. Not out here."

The man smiled, as if he had heard this many times before – but no matter how many times it was said, he knew it was wrong all the same.

"I have made these lands my home for two decades without my sight," the man said. "Every tree, every rock, I know from memory. Men do not pass this way. Not anymore. They have all gone west, or south. The rest were taken by the Blight."

"You are alone?" Samuel asked.

The man nodded. "I am. If you do not believe me, there is nothing I can say to convince you." He gestured to a spot near the fire. "May I sit? These knees are not what they used to be."

Samuel paused, unsure. "Go ahead. We're watching you, though."

"There is no need to fear," the man said, stepping forward. "I simply take food where I can find it, and sleep where I can get it. I am the Wanderer."

Samuel nodded toward Makara. She grimaced, and found a bowl and a spoon for the old man. She ladled some stew in – two healthy scoops. Samuel eyed her. She scowled, and ladled another small scoop in. Satisfied, Samuel nodded again. Makara handed the old man the stew.

Somehow, he knew it was there, because he reached out and took it.

"It's hot," he said, with a smile. "Good."

Everyone watched the old man. Anna was wary and had a hand on her blade the entire time. Personally, I didn't think the old man was any harm. I just wondered what he was doing out here, and how he survived in the wild without his eyesight.

The old man ate several mouthfuls. He did not seem to mind that it was near scalding.

"Who are you?" Samuel asked. "What brings you to our cave?"

The old man chuckled. *"Your* cave?"

Samuel frowned and looked unsure of himself.

"Nothing is anybody's," the old man said. "Not anymore. In the Old World, they had mountains of paper deciding who owned what. All that is irrelevant. In the Old World, I owned some land here, by Mount Elden. I was a very rich man. But I suppose you do not care about that, either."

"I hope you don't mind us staying here," Samuel said.

"Oh, no. It's been so long since anyone has been out this way. I stay away from the city. For a long time, there were people there, even after the Rock fell. They're all gone – either dead, or taken south. I was the only one who stayed."

"Taken?" I asked. "By who? Where?"

"By the Novans," the old man said. "I have talked to their kind before. A group passed this way, about a month ago. Asking about Bunkers."

"How many?" Samuel asked.

"There were six or so," the old man said. "They are long gone, into the Great Blight. Who knows what became of them?"

We all looked at each other. As long as it was not *our* Bunker, Bunker One, there was no problem. But hadn't Marcus said that was on the top of their list?

There was no way to know for sure without asking the man. I didn't think Samuel would want to give that away. Not yet, anyway.

"Why did you stay when everyone else left?" Anna asked.

"This is my home, and I'm far too old for moving. Here I have stayed ever since Dark Day. The government would not let me into Bunker 88, in the mountain. So I made my own bunker. That was long, long ago. Thirty years ago. I would have been fifty."

"What is your name?" I asked.

The man smiled. "I don't remember what it was people called me. I am different. I have been preserved for a purpose. I have seen you coming."

Everyone looked at each other, thinking the old man was crazy.

"But...you can't see," I pointed out.

The man took another bite of stew. He was slowing down, and the bowl was nearly drained.

"This is what I do remember. My family and I survived for nearly a year in my underground bunker. It was a horrible experience. We ended up coming out a year after. My wife, two daughters, and their husbands, and two children. That was 2031. Those days were bad."

The man did not speak for a while. He finished eating.

"I remember watching the sky every night since Ragnarok first became visible. It grew and grew, redder and brighter each night. It is a strange thing to watch your own death approach you and not be able to do anything about it. You cannot imagine the terror of those times. 'The Dark Decade' does not even begin to describe it. It's a wonder the world didn't blow itself up with nuclear war before Dark Day."

"And you have lived out here for all this time?" I asked.

"More or less," the man said. "But I have wandered many places – north, south, west, and east."

"How do you survive?" Samuel asked. "No weapon, no vision...and forgive me for saying, but you're old."

The Wanderer chuckled. "Yes. I am old. Too old for this world, that is for sure. But I have another kind of vision. A vision of the mind, that allows me to see that which needs to be seen; even things that are not visible, such as thought and intent."

"What do you mean?" I asked.

"It was not always this way," the man said. "But I have an inner feeling that I have learned to trust, and it directs me in the right way. Just as it directed me here, to this cave. *Go to the cave,* it said. I did not question. I went. Maybe it is God. Maybe it is something else. It is there, all the same."

"That makes no sense," Makara said.

Samuel held a hand up. "And you are alone?"

The Wanderer gave a single nod. "I have been alone for years. This land is empty. Not even the Raiders come this far. There is no reason. This is the eastern fringe of the Boundless, and beyond that is the Great Blight – where no man goes. I lived in the east, for a time. Now, the Blight is a wall, and east and west will never speak again – unless one were to stop the Blights."

We all looked at each other. This man pinpointed our exact mission, without even knowing us.

He smiled in satisfaction. "Do you believe, now?"

"How do you know the reason we have come?" Samuel asked.

"I know many things, Samuel."

Everyone gasped, but I wasn't convinced. He could have overheard someone saying the name if he had been hiding outside for a while.

"Are you some type of mind reader?" Lisa asked. "I've heard of such people."

"Not so much as that," the Wanderer said. "With my mind, I see many things that are hidden. If I look into your eyes, then I can see your fate."

I was skeptical. "Can you tell us if we'll succeed in our mission?"

The old man didn't say anything to that. "No, I cannot tell you that. No one can. But I can tell you what you must do, or you'll certainly fail."

That got everyone's attention. Everyone waited for the Wanderer to speak.

"What must we do?" Samuel asked.

"Everyone's individual part is different," the Wanderer said. "And I must tell you each in turn. After I've told you, you cannot tell any other person, or it all falls apart."

"Clearly," I said.

Everyone looked at me, urging me to be respectful. It was hard, because I wasn't buying it. I didn't really believe in anything supernatural, but the closest thing that came to it were the Blights and the monsters it spawned.

The Wanderer paid me no heed, however. Instead, he turned to Lisa.

"Lisa." She jumped when he said her name. "You first."

The Wanderer stood, and Lisa looked up at him.

"Now?"

"Yes. Yours is short, but important."

Lisa walked over to the Wanderer. Fear was in her eyes, even if she hid it well in her composure.

The Wanderer spoke softly, and Lisa listened. Whatever the Wanderer said, however important, she kept her face unreadable. He said maybe two sentences before she turned away and sat where she had been before, her face unreadable.

Next, he looked at Samuel. He stood and walked immediately to the Wanderer. The Wanderer drew him away from the fire, toward the mouth of the cave. They talked for a while – maybe five minutes. Samuel asked a question here and there, but was mostly quiet.

It seemed strange to me that these two could soak up this man's words and take them at face value. Who was he? There was no such thing as prophecy or mysticism. There was only science and brute fact. My father had taught me as much. If there was a God, if there was *anything* – why would he have let Ragnarok fall in the first place?

Samuel returned to his spot by the fire. The Wanderer stood, looking at Anna.

She rose and walked forward, as if meeting her death. The Wanderer spoke to her for maybe half a minute – after which she nodded once. She stood there a moment, and then came back. She did not meet my eyes when she sat.

It was just me and Makara. The Wanderer shifted his gaze between us, as if deciding who should go first. Finally, his eyes rested upon Makara.

"Makara."

Makara got up and went to the Wanderer. He spoke to her in much the same way he had spoken to everyone else. I could tell she was fighting back tears. It was not as if the Wanderer had said anything unkind to her – Makara would not have cried about that. It just made me wonder what it was he said.

It was my turn. I was starting to doubt myself. At first, I didn't think this man could see the future, at least no more than I could. Now, I wasn't sure.

I walked past the fire and stood in front of the Wanderer, as the rest had. His eyes were filmy, and for some reason, they spooked me and didn't seem natural. They were cloudy and gray, and seemed to shine in the firelight. Then, I realized why they made me uncomfortable.

They reminded me a bit of the monsters' eyes. For some reason, though, I felt nothing malevolent or evil from the man. In fact, I felt the opposite.

"How are you, Alex?"

"Don't you know that already?"

I shouldn't have been cheeky, but I couldn't help it. The man paid no heed – he only smiled.

"I will tell you something I haven't told the others. It might be the most important thing of all."

I had nothing to say, so I just listened.

"Years ago, after my wife died and my children departed, I became lost in a Blight. It was my custom to take long walks, and I would be gone for days, even weeks at a time. Curiosity got the better of me; I did not realize how dangerous the Blight was at that time, but nothing attacked me. Somehow, though, I lost my way, and night fell. It soon became clear that I would have to settle there for the night. I slept beneath a great, silver tree, and when I awoke...everything was different.

"The most obvious was my blindness. At first, I panicked, but I realized that I could still...*sense* things. It took months to cultivate the ability, but in time, I could get around just as well as I could before...in some cases, even better. Strange memories came to me, things that had never happened to me before. Whenever I saw anyone, I often could see their lives laid before them, as if it were a road. And there were deeper things I knew, things of the heart, that couldn't be put to words.

"That night, I had somehow died and become something else. *Someone* else. And I'm still trying to put the pieces together..."

"None of this makes any sense," I said.

"Sometimes, it doesn't have to make sense."

I tried to make sense of *that* one, but it only left me more confused.

"I will tell you what I can, Alex. All of this is bigger than any of you realize. It will all be made apparent, soon – and all of you must decide what to do with that information. At least, the ones of you who survive. It was written that there will be wars and rumors of wars when the end comes. Maybe the end itself isn't coming – but *an* end surely is."

"You said some will die?"

"Some?" the Wanderer whispered. "Maybe all. As soon as you cross the border into the Great Blight, everything will change. You will be fighting for your very lives, every second, every breath."

"We already are," I said.

"You *think* you are. Something is out there that is far more sinister than the crawlers; far more ancient, far more powerful, far more odious. I see it in my dreams, I hear it in the wind..."

"What is this something?"

"I cannot name it," the Wanderer said. "It is still formless, in my mind, though I'm working to understand it. I can say that this darkness is tied to the meteor, Ragnarok, and it will enslave all life if it cannot be stopped. I have wandered greatly in the Blight, seeking answers. Something tells me that I still have a greater part to play in all this, and every day that passes, I grow more into my role."

The Wanderer paused a moment, as if assessing my reaction. I didn't know what to think of all this, but something about the Wanderer's words rung true. It went beyond logic and reason. It was something I felt in my bones.

"Tomorrow will be your last day on this side, and then you'll arrive at the gateway to the Great Blight. Once you cross over, there will be no going back. It all hinges on you, Alex. You have wondered, more than once, what your place is here, with this group. I am telling you now. Without you, this mission will fail. Without you, the world will fall and everyone will die."

"What are you talking about?" I asked. "Why...why does it all hinge on *me?*"

"I can only say so much, Alex. The rest you will have to discover on your own. Even I cannot see your end. But this I can say: something does not want you reaching Bunker One, and it isn't just the Novans."

"What do I have to do? Just tell me, and I'll do it."

"There is a sacrifice you must make. You'll know it when the time comes."

Sacrifice? That was the last thing I wanted to hear. "I...I can't do that."

"Without suffering, there can be no victory. But take heart: courage can be found in the unlikeliest of places."

"Where will I find mine?"

"A light will come," the Wanderer said. "And you will fight for it even more than you fight for yourself. You have a gift no one else here has, Alex. If this group can't come together, you all might as well leave and return to Raider Bluff to await the inevitable end, because the end *is* coming. I used to think that Ragnarok was the end. No. Ragnarok was only the beginning."

The Wanderer's warning sent chills down my spine.

"Please," I said. "Just clearly tell me what I have to do."

"Listen to your heart. Take courage. The darkness might be deep, but even a single light can push it back. Your potential is far beyond what you even realize, as it is for everyone. Do your best to encourage others when they stumble. There is always something we can do to make another's day brighter – a smile, a kind word or gesture – it's the small things that give us the strength to do the big things."

The Wanderer turned from me and faced the fire, its orange glow reflecting off his face.

I just nodded, not really sure what to say, but it seemed as if the Wanderer was finished. I just turned and went to sit where I was before, not looking at anyone on the way.

The Wanderer sat on the opposite end of the fire, closing his eyes. When he opened them, he spoke, facing all of us.

"Steel yourselves. In two days, everything changes.

Be ever vigilant, not just for those who would attack you...but among yourselves. You can do more for each other than each of you can do for yourselves. The Wanderer smiled. "A case in point; could any of you spare an old man a blanket?"

"I'll bring you one," I said, getting up.

I went to the Recon, and found him something to cover up with. Once I'd grabbed a thick blanket, I returned and handed it to the Wanderer. He took it, wrapped himself up, and lay with his back to the fire. Within moments, his breathing was even with sleep.

No one said much of anything after that. I lay down and wrapped myself in my own blanket, thinking about what he had told me.

It all hinged on me. What did that mean? And I had to sacrifice something, and I would only know that when the time came.

I only hoped it wouldn't be my life.

TWELVE

W hen we awoke the next morning, the Wanderer was gone. He must have left during the night, because the blanket I'd given him was left behind, folded neatly on a nearby rock.

Everyone worked to break camp quickly, packing the Recon with purpose. Anna seemed distant, so I decided to see what was up.

"You okay?"

She paused after spreading the ashes of the night's fire. "It's nothing."

"Nothing always means something, right?"

She looked at me with annoyance, but there was a softness to it, too. "That Wanderer told me something. I guess I can't tell you what it is, since he told me not to, but...it wasn't good news."

"Whatever it was, you'll get through it, right?" I asked.

She smiled sadly. "That's the way it always is." She looked toward the Recon, where everyone else was already getting in.

Makara turned on the engine, and it roared to life in the thin mountain air.

"Time to go," Anna said.

Makara honked the horn, and leaned out the window. "You two, hurry up! We're burning daylight."

We went to the Recon and got into the cab, and a moment later, we set off, leaving the cave behind.

Everyone seemed quiet and contemplative, probably an effect of the Wanderer's visit the night before. Makara kept the Recon on a steady course east, weaving through the dead trees on either side of us. The ground was bare, bereft of life. Above, the red clouds churned, looking especially baleful today. The scene was depressing.

Makara navigated the rocky, dry earth slowly. As the miles passed, I could see we were lowering in elevation. Ahead lay a wide desert vista filled with rocks, dunes, and mountains. A thin line, barely discernible, marked the interstate that headed east. In the far distance the sky was a bit brighter, but the sun was still too weak to force much of its light through.

Samuel pored over the map, his eyes squinting in concentration.

"How's your arm holding up?" I asked.

"Much the same," he said, without looking. "Feels the same as yesterday, and the day before."

"Get on the highway?" Makara asked.

"The highway will take you the rest of the way there. We should be hitting the border of the Great Blight soon."

Anna's words reminded me of the fact that she would not be with us much longer. We still had the rest of the day, and tomorrow morning, before she headed back.

"Are you sure you'll make it back all right on your own?" I asked.

"I can handle myself," she said. "It's not like any of you can come with me, anyway."

I decided to hold my peace, though somehow the prospect of her leaving felt wrong.

The next few hours passed in silence. Everyone was tired, and Samuel and Makara were intent on navigating the Recon.

Ahead were two great rocks the highway passed between. Makara went through the gap.

It was upon leaving the other side that something big pummeled the Recon's side.

The Recon spun out, and Makara slammed on the brakes. When the Recon came to a standstill, we were facing the direction we had come from.

Several creatures with multiple, scuttling legs shot in front of the Recon. They were low to the ground, pink, and looked something like a cross between a scorpion, with their whip-like tails, and a lizard, with their glittering pink scales. They had long faces and snouts filled with dagger-like teeth, along with slits for eyes that glowed white in the dim morning light.

"Crawlers," Anna said.

Makara floored the accelerator, and as she did, two of the crawlers sailed through the air toward the windshield, their long bodies wriggling back and forth. Makara spun to the right, and the crawlers slammed into the Recon's side.

"The turret!" Samuel yelled. "Get to the turret!"

I forced myself up, trying not to crash from all the bumps. I made it to the ladder in the cargo bay and hauled myself up. Hitting the cold desert air was a shock, but I snapped the gun into position and clicked the safety off.

Those crawlers moved fast, and it was hard to get a good mark. There were four of them, and they easily matched the Recon in speed. They scurried across the ground, their forms a blur.

I fired, hitting one of the monsters. It gave a wretched squeal as it tumbled from its own velocity, sliding and rolling through the dirt to its death.

Lisa emerged next to me, sniper rifle in hand.

"Need a hand?"

I didn't answer as I started firing at another one. This one dodged my bullets, but Lisa was already aiming. It would be difficult for her to get a decent shot, but the ground had flattened, so hopefully it would be enough for her to score a hit. Lisa fired, the sound so loud that it temporarily deafened me. One of the crawlers crashed and rolled over, sliding to a stop.

The remaining two backed off, slowing down and allowing the Recon to get away.

"Looks like they're giving up," I said.

Just as I said it, they sped up again, running insanely fast.

"Watch out!" I said, taking aim.

That was when they took to the air, sailing through it, their long mouths open and revealing razor-sharp teeth. They both let out high shrieks as they crashed on top of the cargo bay, their sharp claws clinging to the metal. They scuttled forward like insects.

I aimed for the leftmost one, blasting it right off the Recon. It flew into the air and crashed into the dust.

The other had closed the gap, and was nearly on top of me and Lisa. Its mouth widened, discharging a rancid stench from within. It shimmied over the railing, planting one of its paws on my chest, knocking me back from the gun.

My arms grappled its neck, but it was way too strong. The only thing that stopped it from mauling me was Lisa, who was now stabbing it in its side. It let out a horrible wail before turning to deal with her, kicking and causing her to sprawl over the railing, nearly toppling over. The crawler returned its attention to me.

That was when Anna showed up, her katana flashing. With a scream, she brought her blade down, slicing the crawler's head from its torso, which sent a spray of purple ooze gushing from its neck. I jerked to avoid the stream, and it missed me by inches. The severed head rolled off the side and landed on the ground.

The crawler's weight pressed into me, constricting my breathing.

Anna pushed against the heavy body, grunting from exertion, just enough for me to slink out from under it. By this time, Lisa had rescued herself from falling over the side, panting from exertion.

"That's all of them," Anna said.

Together, we pushed the crawler off the Recon. It tumbled to the dusty ground below.

"Everyone okay?" I asked.

Lisa winced in pain, touching her back. "It slammed me into the railing. I'll be feeling that for a while."

"See if Makara can look at it," I said. "If it's serious..."

"It'll leave a nasty bruise, that's all," Lisa said. "It takes more than that to slow me down."

Anna cleaned her weapon with a rag, wiping her blade clean. Scrunching her nose at the dirty cloth, she threw it over the side.

"I think I'm going to stay up here a while," I said. "There should probably be someone up here to keep watch, anyway."

"I'll let them know everyone's fine," Lisa said. She looked at Anna. "Thanks."

"Don't mention it."

Lisa climbed down the ladder.

Anna looked at me. "You okay?"

"Yeah. I thought I was dead."

"You'll have a lot of moments like that. Until you're dead."

She turned away, her head down. Her black hair blew in the wind.

"Something on your mind?" I asked.

She looked at me, but I couldn't read what she was thinking. For some reason, that look reminded me of Khloe, and I felt as if I'd been kicked in the gut.

"You look like the one with something on their mind."

I nodded, but didn't say anything. She waited for me to speak, but I said nothing. What was there to say? The last thing she wanted to hear was how she reminded me of my dead girlfriend.

"It's nothing."

Anna seemed to accept that, thankfully. Despite how much I didn't want to like Anna, I couldn't help but feel a spark when she was nearby. I hated it, because starting tomorrow morning, I'd never see her again. Not to mention the fact that tomorrow morning, I could be dead.

I didn't know how we were going to cross the Great Blight all the way to Cheyenne, Colorado. Hundreds of miles of Blight seemed impossible to fathom.

The first stretch of our journey had ended. The second, more difficult one, was about to begin.

IT WAS GETTING DARK BY THE TIME WE SAW THE FIRST twisted trees. Seeing them again was a horrifying sight, as it was only a sign of much worse things to come. They were stunted, leafless, and had become vessels of the xenovirus that dripped pink slime.

About a mile to the east was the border of the Great Blight. It was chilling to look at: a giant wall of purple and pink, stretching from north to south, horizon to horizon, maybe as much as one hundred feet high. Its surface glowed in the night, whether from its own bioluminescence, or from absorbing sunlight all day.

Makara pulled to a stop, still a fair distance from the border. Darkness had quickly cloaked the land. Trying to find a way in tonight would be madness.

We were the only blot on the windswept desert flatland, other than the occasional dune.

"We camp here tonight," Samuel said.

We were a little exposed, but anything resembling cover was left twenty miles back. We would just have to risk the threat of attack. I shuddered to think of more crawlers out there in the night. Could they see us? Hear us? Smell us? Or were they waiting for us to cross the border before doing anything else?

Despite my trepidation, nothing happened that night. We all slept soundly, except Samuel and Lisa, who kept watch.

I wondered if this was going to be the last time I ever slept.

THIRTEEN

We left at sunrise after a quick breakfast and headed the final mile to the Great Blight.

It might have been my imagination but it seemed a bit closer than yesterday. Seeing that pink wall stretch from north to south in a near perfect line was damn unnerving. It was as if something had built it. What that something *was,* I didn't know. It was all encoded into the genetics of the xenovirus,

I supposed. If that was the case, the xenovirus was far more complicated than my father had thought.

We approached within a hundred feet of the wall, and we had to crane our necks to see the top of it. The twisting pink, purple, and orange growth was thick, gnarled, interlocking, as if designed to keep people out, or to keep something else *in.* The wall cast a long, pinkish shadow from the low morning sun. There was no telling how thick it was, or how to pass through. Makara turned north, driving the Recon alongside it for a good hour.

At last, there appeared to be an opening.

"There," Samuel said, pointing.

Makara turned. "I don't see anything."

"You can barely see it because the colors play tricks on your eyes. But it's there"

Makara's eyes narrowed, and then she nodded grimly. "Yeah. I see it, now."

I looked at Anna, wondering when she'd be leaving, but her face only appeared troubled.

"You okay?"

"I can't leave," she whispered.

Makara's eyes flicked to the rearview. "What do you mean? That was the agreement."

Anna sighed. "Yeah. I know. But the Wanderer said I would have a choice, and I'm making that choice now. My role here isn't done. Without me, you guys won't make it. If you guys will have me, I'd like to join you the rest of the way to Bunker One."

No one said anything. Samuel turned around.

"You realize what that means, right?"

Anna nodded slowly. "Yeah. I know. We might not be coming back. It's important that I go on, though, and that's my choice. If I don't go...I'll regret it. And so will all of you."

"Well, I don't think anyone else would be against it," Samuel said. Despite his words, I saw Makara scowl. "You're a good fighter and we could use someone with your skills."

"What will Char think?" Makara asked.

"Char will be made to understand, if we ever see him again," Anna said. "This is bigger than Char. This is my chance to follow my true path. No more being a bodyguard. It's time for me to rise up above that."

"Let her come," Lisa said. "Like Samuel said, she'll hold her own. Besides, I don't want to go against what the Wanderer said."

Even Makara couldn't question that, though I could see suspicion written on her face.

"You're really staying, then?" I asked.

She held my gaze. There was no faltering in it.

"Yes. This is my mission, too, now, as much as it is any of yours."

"It's decided, then," Samuel said.

Makara pressed the accelerator, and we rolled forward, toward the entrance of the Great Blight.

MAKARA SLOWED THE RECON AS WE APPROACHED THE break in the wall that led to the purple xenofungus. The opening was a giant archway of fungus, a gateway left intentionally open for creatures to enter and leave. It was empty, now, as far as I could see, and as the Recon transferred from the hard rock to the soft fungus, the ride became eerily smooth. The fungus sloped upward in a wide ramp, and on either side were tall, organic walls, twisted and dripping with slime. The tunnel cast colorful shadows on the vehicle, filtering through the windows and lighting everything in a pinkish hue.

Now that we were in, I wanted back out. The puffy fungus extended up the hill, its bewildering, multicolored hues not easy on the eye. Twisted columns rose from the ground, spreading in a series of hanging tubes that all dripped slime. The slime collected at the bases of the columns, forming pools and icky streams. Clouds of insects swarmed above the pools.

A couple minutes into the Great Blight, I could feel the hostility of the landscape. I used to think we weren't coming back. Now, I knew. The Wanderer was right; something dark was behind all this. It went beyond the xenovirus and Ragnarok.

But that was why we were here. We had to figure out why this was happening and how to stop it.

Finally, we made it to the top of the incline, and it

was hard not to be depressed at the sight. In all directions was something that could only be described as a xenofungal forest. There were thousands upon thousands of xenotrees, alien to behold, spreading in all directions. The trees' foliage was afire with blinding orange, shining from the feeble rays of sun that found their way through the red-clouded sky. The trees grew so thick that it seemed impossible that we could ever get through them. They extended to the far horizon and there was no telling where they ended. That is, *if* they ended. Some of the trees were tall – maybe a hundred feet high – and the biggest ones had offshoots of their own that connected to other trees in a spidery labyrinth. I thought of the creatures that had attacked us, and how many would be lurking within that jungle.

We would be reduced to a crawl if we went through, if we didn't get stuck altogether. The Recon's speed would be of no advantage. It was a good thing the Recon had a compass, or we would surely get lost in that maze.

No one said anything for a long time. I seriously wondered whether Makara was going to turn back.

Only she didn't do that.

"Kind of makes you wish we could fly, huh?"

She drove down the hill toward the forest.

WHEN WE ENTERED THE FIRST LINE OF TREES, THE ENTIRE sky was nearly blocked out. Makara turned on the headlights, revealing a web of trees and branches. Soon, the strange growth became so thick that it was less like a forest and more like a cave. We didn't find anything living other than the plants – at least, not yet. It seemed as if something was waiting to jump out from around every bend.

At points, the slime dripped and splattered onto the windshield. The washer fluid and wipers could only get so much off. The rest stuck in a thin film that, while not impossible to see out of, made the windshield a bit blurry.

We continued for an hour like this, crashing through the undergrowth and avoiding the trees. Nobody spoke. The landscape darkened, becoming more twisted, dark, and terrifying.

Through the windshield, a small circle of natural light materialized in the distance, like the exit of a cave.

"I think that's the way out," Makara said.

I checked the compass, seeing that we were still heading east. The circle of light grew in size over the next few minutes. The Recon's headlights illumined the thick, gnarled tree trunks embedded in the xenofungus, their roots plunging into the surface like tentacles.

We emerged from the forest and everyone heaved a sigh of relief. We had entered the Great Blight's equivalent of a meadow – a wide, open space carpeted by the pink and purple xenofungus, flanked on all sides by the grotesque trees. The clearing was only a temporary escape from the xenoforest, but all the same, it was good to see the sky again, even if it was its usual menacing red.

In the center of the meadow, Makara pulled to a stop. It was midday, and we had probably only gotten ten miles closer to our goal.

"I hope it's not all like this," Makara said. "I just need a minute."

That was when I saw something moving in the trees. "Guys..."

Everyone looked toward the south, where I was pointing. There were dozens of crawlers appearing from the trees in all directions. Some were big, some small – but all of them had those white orbs for eyes. Their wails and screeches pierced the air, sending chills down my spine.

"*Go!*" Samuel said.

The Recon's engine roared, and the monsters charged.

Everyone in the backseat headed for the turret. Lisa climbed up the ladder first, followed by me, then Anna. By the time I emerged at the top, Lisa was firing.

I could see the eastern edge of the jungle approaching, where a narrow trail led further east, flanked on both sides by blighted trees.

If we could get on that trail, there would be no need to go back into the jungle.

Makara veered the Recon in that direction, even as a stream of monsters fell in behind, keeping pace. Lisa continued to fire as we entered the path, the monsters tumbling over each other in a mad attempt to get to us. The creatures screamed as the powerful bullets entered them. She swung the gun back and forth, doing whatever she could to stop the wave, but there were so many that it had almost no effect. The ones who fell were only buried and trampled as the rest stampeded over them.

The trail weaved back and forth. Anna tumbled, falling toward the side. I grabbed her and pulled her back to the center of the turret.

Out of the corner of my eye, something pink flew through the air. I turned to see a long-limbed creature dropping from a tree above.

"Look out!"

The monster crashed on top of the cargo bay, making a dent in the roof. When it turned, I could see it had long arms and legs and was ripped from head to toe with muscle. Its shape resembled a gorilla, but who knew what it had been before? It had no hair and its sickly pink skin was coated in slime. The way those white orbs burned gave me chills.

Anna drew her katana while I took out my Beretta, aiming for the monster's head. As it hurtled forward, I fired three times. Two of the bullets entered its shoulder while the third missed. It roared in pain, but used its opposite arm to swipe, extending its long claws outward.

I ducked just in time, and so did Anna. Lisa swung the turret to face the creature, opening fire.

Even over the din, I could hear the creature's roar. I covered my ears as the monster fell backward, crashing onto the fungus-covered ground below. The crawlers overran the monster's body like a raging river.

My ears rang and my head felt as if it were going to split open.

Lisa hopped off the turret. "We can't stay up here. There's too many."

Anna was already descending the ladder, followed by me. Lisa came last, slamming the hatch shut above her and locking it tight. I could hear the rattle and scuttle of legs on the cargo bay above.

It wasn't looking good at all.

We went into the cab, shutting ourselves out from the cargo bay. I doubted the creatures could storm it, but if they put enough weight on the Recon, they could grind it to a halt.

Makara swerved back and forth, which seemed to dislodge a few of the creatures. I saw them fall in the LCD, even as more readied to jump.

"We can't keep up like this," Makara said. "We'll have to fight them eventually."

We left the trail, finding that the forest had suddenly ended. Before us spread a large, open valley of pink and purple, pockmarked with gnarled trees. Mountains surrounded the valley on all sides. There was something strange rising from the center of the depression. At first, it looked like a tall, thin mesa, coated in pink fungus.

But as we got closer, I saw that it wasn't a mesa. There were rectangles along the outside surface, faded beneath a fungal shell.

It was a skyscraper, out in the middle of nowhere.

"Head for the building," Samuel said. "We'll make our stand there."

FOURTEEN

As Makara drove toward the building, it was as if the ground itself came alive. Monsters squirmed their way through the xenofungus, charging for the Recon. Makara swerved left and right to avoid them, all the while making for the tall building. The creatures leaped through the air, crashing into the windshield and rolling off to the side. Purple blood splattered the glass. Makara turned on the wipers, but that only made it worse.

"Can't see a damn thing," she said.

"We're almost there," Lisa said. "Just keep going!"

A few seconds more, and the windshield had sufficiently cleared to see again. The building was getting close. It was tall, and completely out of place in this secluded valley.

"Pull in there!" Samuel said, pointing to an opening in the ground. "Looks like an underground garage."

"Who knows what could be down there?" Makara asked. "But it's our only option."

She pulled into the opening and the creatures

followed us down. Makara turned on the headlights, revealing the road spiraling down to the left.

Where the road straightened, we were greeted by rows and rows of parked cars; cars that had likely been here since Dark Day, thirty years ago. Most were buried beneath a thin layer of fungus, which encased them all in a single cocoon. The Recon's headlights lit the fungus-covered ceiling, illuminating upside-down tiny creatures that scattered in every direction.

"Not looking good," Makara said.

"There's a door over there," Samuel said. "It should lead inside. Park in front of it and then we can use the Recon as a shield to block them from coming after us."

Makara made for the door, parking the Recon sideways against it and killing the engine.

"Everyone out!" Samuel shouted. "Move, move, *move!*"

"Through my door," Makara said, "unless you want to get killed."

Makara opened her door and stepped out, after which she opened the door into the building. The rest of us crawled into the front seat and exited through the driver's side door. The trail of crawlers had caught up with us, but they were delayed by the Recon's position. It would give us a few more seconds to get out before they circumvented it.

Makara was already inside the building, and the rest of us followed her in, Lisa bringing up the rear with her sniper rifle. She shut the Recon's door, heading inside with the rest of us. Samuel slammed the building door behind us, shutting out the monsters and their horrible cries. I heard the click of a lock, and it was only a few seconds more until I heard the crawlers pushing against it.

"That should hold them," Samuel said. "At least, for a while.

The building's interior was pitch black and cold. Several flashlights clicked on; apparently, some of us had remembered to grab our tote backpacks. I had nothing but my gun, my knife, and my canteen. It was too late now, though. We were effectively cut off from everything that still lay in the Recon.

The lights revealed a dark, dingy hallway, and not much else.

"What now?" Makara asked.

"I don't know," Samuel said. "Let me think."

"We should probably get higher up," Lisa said. "It would be safer. Maybe we can wait them out."

"Good idea," Samuel said. "We can find a room and secure it. Tomorrow...we can check on the Recon."

"We still don't even know if this building is secure," Anna said.

"It's too large to survey," Samuel said. "We just need to secure a small area."

"We should get moving," Lisa said. "We're wasting time."

Samuel took the lead, shining a flashlight with his good arm. Makara followed behind, alongside Lisa. Both had their pistols out, while Anna drew her katana, being careful to be quiet about it. Bringing up the rear, I drew my Beretta.

No one said a word as Samuel led us up a stairwell on our right. The sounds of our footsteps clanging in the darkness shattered the silence.

We had gone up four flights of steps when we heard a gunshot, distant.

Samuel held up a hand, and cocked his head to listen. We waited one, two, three seconds. Nothing.

"Someone else is here," Lisa said, voice low.

"Whoever they are, they probably know *we're* here," Samuel said. "And we brought a whole army of monsters to their doorstep."

"Other survivors?" Makara asked.

Another shot rang out, deafening loud, and a bullet dinged off the metal step below me. As more shots filled the air, I heard Samuel yell above the din.

"Run!"

We ran upstairs. Footsteps, yells, and more shots followed us from below. There were at least three or four of them, but they had the element of surprise. I charged upward, rounding the bends of the stairs. I lost count of the flights, but within a couple of minutes, we were on the top floor. Samuel ran across the hall, throwing a metal door open. Everyone followed him in, and I was the last one through. A bullet zinged off the door, and I slammed it shut just in time, finding the latch and locking it in place.

We had entered a dim room that contained a desk piled with papers, a file cabinet, a trash can, and a broken computer. Pink and faded sunlight filtered through the fungus-tinged window, tinting the room and its items with an eerie pink glow.

"We're trapped," Lisa said.

I heard voices from the other side of the doorway. A moment later, a male voice could be heard from the other side.

"Who are you? And what are you doing here?"

"I could ask you the same," Samuel said, his voice carrying.

"You don't own this place. This is our territory, and you're violating it."

"Look," Samuel said, "I don't know who you think you are, but those things are out there and we had nowhere else to go. If you're telling us to leave, you're just going to have to make us. It's five against however many you have, and we all have guns. Your call."

That shut the man up. I heard two more voices whispering out there.

"There's no point in fighting," Samuel said, taking advantage of the silence. "We don't want to harm you, and we hope you don't want to harm us. We'll just wait for these things to go away and we'll be out of your hair."

"Those monsters you brought here....they're not leaving."

"We had no choice!" Samuel yelled. "What would you expect me to do, drive out there until they over-whelmed us?"

"That would have been nice," the man said.

"I'm tired of this," Lisa said, taking out her handgun. "Let's just kill them while we can."

Apparently, the man outside heard that. "That door moves so much as an inch, we're firing."

"Lisa, take it easy," Samuel said. "Let me handle this." Samuel turned back to the door. "Maybe we can work together."

"I want to know who you are first, Raider."

"We aren't Raiders," Samuel said.

"You're Wastelanders with guns and attitudes. That makes you Raiders to me."

"We're on a mission sanctioned by the United States government," I said.

That made the man go quiet. There were more whispers.

"There is no U.S. government," the woman said. "All the Bunkers are gone."

Maybe that was true. Two of the remaining four had fallen in the last month, including Bunker 108, which had once been my home.

"Not all of them," I said.

"Who are you with?" Samuel asked. "The Empire?"

There was a short moment of silence.

"It doesn't matter who we're with," the man snapped. "We're asking the questions."

"We have more guns," Samuel said. *"We* ask the questions."

"You're locked in," the man said. "I'd like to see how your 'more guns' works out."

"This is pointless," I said, loud enough for only us to hear. "We need to get them on our side somehow so we can get out of here. Empire or not, all of us are surrounded by an army of monsters."

"What if they're going after the Bunker, too?" Lisa asked. "You remember what the Wanderer said."

"I'm working on that," Samuel said. "But we can't appear weak."

Samuel turned back to the door.

"We're not getting anywhere by fighting. We need to work together. As soon as we can clear these monsters off, the sooner we can leave."

The man laughed. "Clear them off? Maybe you haven't noticed, but there are thousands of them out there. You're stuck here, just like us. Coming into the Great Blight was a mistake. A mistake for *all* of us."

"How many of you are out there?" Samuel asked.

"We're not saying," the man said.

"Less than us, then. If you were more, I'm sure you'd be telling me that."

There was a pause. Apparently, Samuel was right.

"We're three," a woman said. "There's me, and then there's Drake. He doesn't talk much."

A deep grunt answered that statement – I assumed it was Drake.

"Fighting is pointless. Together, we might figure out a way to bring those monsters down."

"You want to team up with someone who opened fire on you?"

Samuel paused. "Not really. What do you suggest we do, then, kill each other off? We really don't have much choice if we both want to live."

There was a long silence, broken only by the group's muted whispering.

"What do you guys think?" Samuel asked us.

"You're right," Makara said. "We don't have much of a choice. I'm letting you know now that my hand isn't leaving my gun."

"Me neither," Lisa said.

Anna and I both nodded our agreement.

At last, the man outside gave us his answer.

"You're right. There's no point in fighting. I'm sorry about opening fire, earlier. We've...we've been stuck here for a while, and we're probably a bit jumpier than we should be."

"Can I trust you to stay calm if I open this door?"

"We won't try anything," the man said. "As long as you promise to do the same."

"We won't," Samuel said. "You have my word."

There was silence for a moment, before the man answered.

"Fine. We're ready when you are."

"All right," Samuel said. "My gun's at my side, and I'm opening the door."

He turned to us, signaling us to be ready for anything. He unlatched the door with a clang. After taking a deep breath, he pulled it open.

For a few seconds, nothing happened. There was a moment of tension as we all watched to see what happened next. There were no shots; only a silence that seemed to stretch far longer than it should have.

A hand reached across the door's threshold.

"I'm Harland," the man said. "This here is Kris, and the big guy is Drake."

Samuel didn't react much, not taking the offered hand. "I'm Samuel. There's Makara, Lisa, Anna, and Alex."

Samuel looked at us, motioning us to stand by the door.

Makara holstered her pistol, and the rest of us followed her lead. Lisa put her handgun away with a scowl while Anna sheathed her katana.

Now that the door was open, I saw what each of them looked like. Harland was a black man, well-muscled and garbed in desert camo. He looked more government than I did. An AR-15 was slung across his back, and his face carried a hard and determined expression. Kris was a short and pretty woman with blonde hair and blue eyes, also dressed in desert camo. Drake was large, muscular, and white as a ghost, wearing a stained white tank top and camo pants. He had two pistols holstered on either side, and curiously, three long javelins pointing up from his back. His left arm bore a tattoo with simple Roman numerals: "XIII." His face was tough, solid, and carried several deep scars.

They were sizing us up, too. I'm sure they thought I wasn't tough, based off my age, but I had learned a lot in the past three weeks.

"How long have you guys been here?" Samuel asked.

"Two weeks," Kris said, shaking a blonde bang out of her eye. "And we've been trying to figure out how to get out ever since. The land will look empty, but every time we try to leave, *they* come back."

"You guys are Imperials, then?" Samuel asked.

The three looked at each other for a moment.

"Yeah, we are," Harland said. "No point in trying to hide it. Mercenaries, really, hired on a job we're not allowed to disclose"

"Bunker crawlers, are you?" Samuel asked.

"What does it matter?" Harland asked, annoyed. "I can see you guys are the same. There's no other reason for you to be here. I don't know if you are working for the United States like you say, but whatever *we* find in the Bunker is ours."

Anna, Lisa, and Makara stepped forward, reaching for their weapons. The three Novans backed off, reaching for theirs.

"Stop!" I said. "You're going to kill each other, over what? No one's making it to the Bunker anyway unless we work together."

"Well," Harland said, "the Bunker isn't far. Just downstairs, in fact. But I'm sure if you're here, you already knew that."

"Wait," Samuel said. "What do you mean, right downstairs?"

Once again, the Novans looked at each other, confused. An uncomfortable silence hung over the two groups.

"Yeah," Harland said. "The door's in the basement, only we can't figure out how to get it open."

Surely, Harland couldn't mean what I thought he meant. Bunker One was in Cheyenne Mountain, hundreds of miles away.

"What door?" Samuel asked.

"They don't know, Har," Kris said.

"Well, they will now. It's the entrance to Bunker 40. It's sealed tight, and there's nothing we can do to get it open."

"No one home, then," I said.

Harland shot me an annoyed look before turning back to Samuel. "If we could somehow bust that thing open, we might have a shot of getting out of here. There could be another exit that will give us a chance to escape. There might even be Recons."

"No harm in us taking a look," Samuel said.

"No chance of blowing that thing up," I said. "It was designed to withstand a lot more than we can throw at it."

I noticed Drake was staring at me. If he was trying to intimidate me, it wasn't working. I stared back.

"Alex," Samuel said. "You're from 108. Any ideas on how to get it open?"

I shook my head. "Unless they're opened from the inside, there's no way to get in. That's their design."

"So we're really stuck here," Makara said. "Still hundreds of miles left to go."

Makara realized her slip, but showed nothing on her face to reveal it. If the Novans caught it, they'd know we weren't here for Bunker 40, but something else entirely.

"Where are you headed?" Harland asked casually.

"That's classified," Samuel said. "Besides, even if there was a way out through Bunker 40, we'd still need to get to our Recon. There would be no way to cross the distance we need without one."

"Recon, huh?" Harland said. "You guys've got lots of fancy toys. Maybe you really are government after all."

"They came from the garage," Kris said. "Is that where you're parked?"

"Might be easier to clear it," Harland said.

"It's probably too dangerous, at least for the moment," Samuel said. "I'd rather take a look at this Bunker." Samuel paused. "What about this building? Is it secure?"

"Well, we've been here for two weeks and we're still alive, for what it's worth."

That was apparently good enough for Samuel.

"Samuel's right," Anna said. "We could at least try to get into the Bunker. There will be lots of useful equipment in there. Maybe we can find something, even if there's no other way out."

"Let's try to figure this out, then," Harland said. "Hopefully, you'll have more luck than us."

FIFTEEN

Harland led us downstairs, our footsteps echoing off the cold walls. I could hear the muffled wails and screams of the monsters outside. I tried not to think what would happen if those thousands of creatures somehow found their way in.

We reached the ground floor, but still, Harland kept going down. As we descended, the air grew wet and dank, and once we reached the bottom, we followed Harland down a dark hallway. Our footsteps splashed through puddles. This would be the perfect time for them to ambush us, so I kept my hand near my handgun.

The corridor opened into a large room, and we shined our flashlights around it. The room was empty and square-shaped with gray brick walls. The only feature of any importance was a large, circular vault door made of thick metal that was set into the wall. The number 40 was impressed in its center. The door was smooth, with no mark or scratch on it, nor did it have any handle. The crack between door and wall was so small and exactly measured that even a thin card could barely fit in the space.

"This is it," Harland said. "Bunker 40."

Samuel stepped forward and placed his hand on the smooth metal, not saying a word.

"Any ideas on how to open it?" Makara asked.

I walked up to the door, joining Samuel. There was no secret way to open the door – at least, not that I knew about. Like Samuel, I ran my hand across the cold metal, as if that might give me some clue. Everyone looked at me as if I were performing some sort of magic spell.

"These things were designed to never be opened," I said. "Except from the inside."

My statement was met with silence. I looked around the door, and noticed a camera sitting above the bunker door. Its lens gazed down at me.

I pointed to it. "That still work?"

Harland shrugged. "I'd be surprised if it did. We've tried talking into it, but nothing happened."

I looked into the camera. Bunker 108 had a similar camera, though it was not as conspicuous as this one. Ours had been built into the rock, and couldn't be seen by the casual observer. The camera was how the doorman knew whom to let in.

If there was a doorman at Bunker 40, I had to try speaking to him.

"Bunker 40," I said to the camera, "this is Alex Keener, son of Dr. Steven Keener, of Bunker 108 in the Mojave Sector. If anyone is in there, we're on a mission from the United States government, sanctioned by Chief Security Officer Chan." I paused, and waited for a response, if any. When nothing happened, I continued. "We're trying to find Bunker One. We're surrounded by monsters on all sides, and we could use your help. If anyone is in there, please, open the door. We're not hostile. We only need your help."

I didn't know what else to say. I knew Samuel didn't

want me to give away the mission, but if this was our only shot of getting inside the Bunker, I had to say the right words that would get them to open the door.

"This isn't working," Makara said. "No one's in there."

"We're looking for the Black Files," I said. "We want to stop the xenovirus."

"Alex," Samuel said sternly. "Enough."

I had given away our mission, and the Bunker door *still* wasn't opening. I felt like a complete fool.

"Well," Harland said, "looks as if you won't be getting those Black Files. Whatever they are."

"It doesn't matter," I said. "We're trapped in here."

At that moment, a loud thump sounded from the door, causing me to jump back. A thunderous echo reverberated throughout the room. Anna crouched beside me, drawing her katana. The echo faded, and the door remained still.

"It's opening," Kris whispered.

From the other side of the Bunker door, I could hear a low screech as the wheel on the other side turned. A cold sweat bathed my skin. Now that it *was* opening, for some reason, I didn't want it to.

"Be ready for anything," Samuel said.

The wheel stopped turning, and the room went quiet. All I could hear were the breaths of the seven people around me, weapons drawn and ready. The circular vault door cracked open with a groan, revealing a sliver of darkness within. A wave of fetid, stinking air issued from the gap, like the opening of a fresh crypt.

Stumbling from the darkness came two human forms. One was male, and one was female, their forms rotted and coated with slime. Their clothes were in tatters, revealing their pale nakedness. They screeched as they shot forward, reaching for me with gnarled, clawed hands.

"Howlers!" Samuel yelled.

I raised my Beretta at the male, right as his open mouth went for my neck. I fired, opening a hole in his forehead. His body fell backward as brain matter spewed from the opposite end of his skull, plastering the Bunker door. He crumpled to the ground in a heap.

The woman went after Anna, who sidestepped her deftly. Anna slashed the Howler woman in the back with her curved blade. With her boot, Anna stomped on the Howler woman's back, rendering her immobile. Anna stabbed downward, right below the base of the woman's skull. The Howler woman went still.

Six more Howlers poured from the open door. Shots were fired, and one of them was immediately felled. But two, one a man and another a child, snuck by and tackled Kris. She screamed as they buried their faces in her neck, ripping out gobbets of flesh. Blood spewed into the air as her screams became bloody gurgles.

Harland pulled one of the monsters off Kris as Anna came forward to sever the adult male's head from its body with a clean, expert swipe. Lisa handled the child Howler with a look of revulsion on her face, stabbing it in the back of the neck with her combat knife.

In front of me, Drake dealt with two Howlers on his own. He pulled a javelin from his quiver and launched it, spearing the head of both Howlers at once. Together, they crashed to the floor.

I faced another Howler, a fat male with blackened veins beneath his pink, cadaverous skin. His wide-open white eyes bored into me as he unleashed a baleful roar that reeked of rot. I aimed carefully for his head, and fired, sending him sprawling to the floor.

Samuel dispatched the last Howler with a shot from his handgun.

All of this happened in seconds, and now, the

Howlers were bloating. It wouldn't be long before they exploded.

"Run!" I yelled.

Kris convulsed on the floor as the rest of us ran for the hallway to take shelter from the pending blasts. Drake was the last one out of the blast zone, and as soon as he had rounded the bend, two plops sounded from the room, followed by several more. Walls of purple slime shot by, splattering against the brick walls and filling the room with a horrible reek that nearly made me heave.

We waited. When we were sure the bodies were done rupturing, we went back to survey the damage. Mangled, torn bodies littered the room, along with pieces of flesh, bone, and organ that had been propelled by the explosions. The stench was unbearable, one of raw sewage and organic rot.

"Kris..." Harland said.

Harland ran from us. We followed him back to the entrance of the Bunker, ready for more to come out. For now, that entrance was quiet as the grave. Kris was still convulsing, blood coursing from the bite wounds on her neck.

Samuel looked grim. "There's nothing we can do for her."

Harland was quiet, his eyes burning and unaccepting of the facts.

"She's infected with the xenovirus," I said. "When she bleeds out...she'll become one of them."

"Let me take care of it," Makara said. "Before more of those things come out."

Harland's eyes narrowed at her with hatred. "Stay away from her."

"Harland," Samuel said. "Kris is *gone*. I'm sorry, but it's the truth."

Harland said nothing, his eyes dark and vengeful. Anna stepped forward.

"Leave this to the pros," she said.

With that, she arced her blade down in a whir. Kris's head was promptly sliced off.

Harland roared, turning to Anna. Drake ran forward, grabbing Harland's arms with his meaty hands.

"Boss," he said in his deep bass voice, "calm down."

Harland was livid. It looked as if he wanted nothing more than to murder Anna.

"I did what I had to," Anna said. "She could have come back any minute as one of them."

"Won't she explode?" Makara asked.

I shook my head. "They have to come back to life, first. It's when they get the white eyes that you've got to be careful."

"How do you know that?" Samuel asked.

"Because my friend died before she turned. She..." It was hard to make myself go on. I tried not to think about Khloe, but it was hard. "One of those things bit her back in 108. She died, but I buried her before she turned."

I left the rest unsaid. I didn't want to bring that nightmare up again. I didn't want to think of her buried in the harsh red sand outside Bunker 108. I had made sure that would never happen, but still, I doubted.

"Well, I'll trust you on that," Samuel said. He eyed everyone, including Harland and Drake. "I need you two to help. I don't know how many of these Howlers are in here, but I need fighters. Are you two good to do that?"

"You're going in there?" Harland asked. "After all of this?"

"I'll do whatever it takes to get my team and myself out of here. If you two want to be a part of that, I suggest you help out. You can grieve for your dead later, but *everyone* will be dead unless we can find an escape."

Drake scowled, but looked to Harland for direction. Harland didn't say anything for a long while. At last, he nodded grimly.

"Lead on, then."

I didn't want to question Samuel. I really didn't. I couldn't contradict him in front of these two. But if what happened at Bunker 108 was any indication, we had no shot at clearing this place out.

"After you guys," Harland said. "Drake and I will bring up the rear."

"That's fine," Samuel said. "Just do your job."

In a swift movement, Drake retrieved his javelin. The two Howlers it had pierced crumpled further to the floor. He gave a sneer of a smile, but Samuel ignored it, pushing himself into the darkness of the bunker.

We all followed.

SIXTEEN

My stomach twisted as we entered the dark Bunker. With the smell of rot intermixed with the sting of metal, it was hard not to think of that horrible night that had changed my life forever.

The atrium looked about the same as the one in my old home. There was a half-circular desk close by the right wall. That was where Deborah Greene would have sat, back in 108. Deborah was dead, along with everyone else in Bunker 108. I half-expected ghosts to float down the halls.

There was a thick metal door behind the desk. I knew what lay beyond it.

"Might not have to go too far after all," I said. "That door leads to the armory."

"Nice work," Samuel said.

Makara hopped over the desk, and gave the door a try. The latch wouldn't budge.

"Figures," she said.

Harland had wandered from the group, and was shining his light on a directory built into the wall.

"This might help," he said.

Everyone gathered around the map. This bunker was larger than 108 – I could see that much. It had seven levels – 108 had five – but the layout was much the same. Cafeteria. Commons. Dormitories. An Officers' Wing. Hydroponics and fusion reactor on the bottom floor.

There was one major difference – there were no labs. Instead, a long tunnel led to the edge of the directory, cutting off there. An arrow pointed upward, off the map. Beside the arrow was the word, "Hangar."

"Hangar?" Anna asked. "Was this place an airport?"

"Could be," I said. "Each Bunker had a specialization. Both 108 and 114 were medical and research oriented. I don't know Bunker 40's designation, but this could have been where planes were kept."

"Would be nice, just to fly out of here," Harland said.

"Nice thought," Lisa said. "But none of us can fly."

Harland turned to her, eyeing her up and down. "Now, you're not bad-looking. What's your name?"

Lisa shot him a venomous glare. "Done grieving already?"

Harland grinned unashamedly. Lisa turned away with a disgusted look.

"What now?" Makara asked.

"The armory's accessible from the Officers' Wing as well," Samuel said, turning from the map. "So that's where we'll go. We can resupply whatever we didn't have time to grab from the Recon. After that, we can find a way out." He gestured down the hall. "Let's move."

As we walked the deserted corridors, I noticed that the Bunker was surprisingly clean for something that had been infected with the xenovirus. No xenofungus stained the wall, as it had in Bunker 114. There was only the foreboding smell of decay that promised more trouble ahead.

We came to an intersection. Samuel pointed left, and we followed him.

We walked deeper into the cold bunker, our flashlights bouncing off the walls and corners. It felt as if we were being watched, or that Howlers were waiting around every end. The fact that we couldn't see anything past our flashlight beams only made it worse. Only the smell promised more trouble ahead.

Soon we stood before an arch in the hallway. Bold letters above read "Officers' Wing." Hopefully, we could find what we were looking for here.

Samuel motioned me to take the lead. The layout of 40's Officers' Wing was basically the same as 108's. There were some slight differences I couldn't explain, but felt.

I pointed to a nondescript metal door on the left. This one stood half open.

"This is it."

We turned the corner. Half the guns had been looted, but there was still plenty of firepower left.

"Jackpot," Makara said.

In addition to the assortment of handguns and rifles, there were also batons, body armor, grenades, heavy machine guns, submachine guns, and plenty of ammunition to boot. There were also empty packs, which each of us grabbed to load up. I started with the 9-millimeter ammo.

"Grab all you can," Samuel said.

The plethora of guns before us was tempting, but I liked my Beretta. It felt right in my hands and I wouldn't dream of replacing it.

It was then that I noticed something was off.

"Wait," I said.

"What is it?" Samuel asked.

All at once, we realized Harland and Drake were missing.

"*Hey!*"

Samuel's voice boomed into the corridor outside. He ran out, pistol in hand. He scanned left and right, then looked back at us.

"They're gone!"

We hurried out of the armory. Down the hall, I could see an open door. I could have sworn it had been closed just a minute ago. A stairway led down into darkness.

"What the hell are they doing?" Samuel asked.

"I don't know," Lisa said. "Maybe they went on without us."

"I'm not leaving anyone behind...even those two."

"They left *us* behind," I said. "They're setting up a trap. I guarantee it."

"Just let me think," Samuel said.

"No," I said. "Let *me*. They're trying to trick us, plain and simple." Everyone looked at me. "They want us to go after them so they can ambush us."

Before anyone could respond, we heard two screams coming from the direction of the stairs.

"Just leave them there to rot," Makara said. "Shut the door, bar it, and find another way out."

"I said, *no!*" Samuel said. "No one deserves to be left in here. Not even them."

Anna brushed a strand of hair from her eye. "Fine. But I think we're making a mistake. Let's just finish this quickly."

"Lead away," Lisa said.

Samuel strode toward the open door, and pointed his gun down the stairwell. Makara came from behind and shined her flashlight down. The light revealed nothing but thirty to forty steps descending into a dark, claustrophobic corridor. I knew going down was a bad idea, but I kept my mouth shut.

Samuel started down, and the rest of us followed, our feet clanging off the metal. The stench of death became more pungent as we descended. When we reached the bottom of the steps, the odor of death in the cold air was nearly unbearable. The corridor opened up into a room.

"Quiet," Samuel muttered.

The three flashlight beams shot around the chamber, revealing the vertical metal bars of prison cells. We were in the detention center. This one was much larger than the one in Bunker 108, and more primitive. There were twelve cells, six on either side.

And all of them were piled with corpses.

"We need to turn back," I said.

The door above slammed shut and locked from the outside. The slamming echo thundered throughout the cells.

The bodies stirred, convulsed, and began writhing like worms in their piles. The ones that broke free shambled up and charged for the bars, their white eyes glowing and soulless.

"Hold your fire!" Samuel said. "As long as they're in there they can't hurt us."

His voice was barely audible above the din of groans. The Howlers slammed into the bars and doors like wild animals.

One of the cell doors crashed open. Several Howlers lumbered out, moving as fast as their unsteady legs could carry them. Another door crashed open, flooding more Howlers into the corridor. They howled in unison, moving as one toward us.

"Fire!" Samuel ordered.

We unleashed our bullets into the infected Howlers. They roared in pain as the bullets entered their chests, their necks, and their heads. They dropped, one by one, but more were coming out of the cells. I switched out my magazine, and resumed firing.

The first to fall were already bloating.

"Back!" Samuel said.

We moved as far from the bodies as we could, the first of them exploding by the time we reached the stairs. We were well out of range of the blast zone, but we were running out of space to retreat into.

"Fire!" Samuel yelled. "They can't get close to us! They have to fall where they stand!"

We fired without abatement, the sound deafening in the room's narrow confines. About two dozen bodies lay piled on the floor before us. More were inflating.

"Back again!"

We retreated up the steps as the bodies exploded, sending streams of goo sailing for the bottom of the stairs. The smell was like raw sewage, and it was all I could do not to gag.

"I think that's all of them," Makara said.

That was when the heavy sound of breathing filled the chamber, along with the deep thud of footsteps.

"What the hell is that?" I asked.

That was when a giant, freakishly large Howler appeared at the bottom of the stairs. He was at least eight feet tall and twice as wide as a normal man. His thick muscles bulged under thin pink skin. His head was hairless, and his eyes burned like white fire. It was a Behemoth, but smaller than Kari and the one we had killed in the canyon. That said, it would still be difficult to handle.

Samuel charged forward with a yell. He pointed his gun at the giant's face, firing into the monster. Even then, the Behemoth didn't slow. It reached for Samuel, grabbing him by the neck. It roared in his face, revealing rows of yellow, razor-sharp teeth.

Samuel aimed right into the giant Howler's mouth, and fired.

The creature groaned, and loosened its grip. It tumbled to the floor, landing at Samuel's feet with a crash.

I looked behind. There was nowhere left to run.

I watched in horror as the thing inflated, the liquid surging beneath the skin, building pressure. This one was going to be so much worse than the others, and the coming explosion threatened to turn us all into these horrible monsters.

SEVENTEEN

"R un!" Makara yelled.

Everyone ran forward past the giant and all the bodies that had just exploded. The entire floor was soaked with purple slime. I slipped across, only saved from falling by Anna catching hold of me.

Then, the Behemoth exploded. I kept running, the tail end of the slime splattering where my feet had been just a second before.

I slid to a stop in front of the others.

"Did anyone get hit?" Samuel asked.

Everyone shook their heads.

"Let's go, then." Samuel said. "We don't have another moment to lose."

"Where are we going?" Lisa asked. "We're barred in."

"We're going forward. That's the only way left to us."

As we followed Samuel into the darkness, I could only wonder what motivated Harland and Drake to betray us like that.

The answer came when Lisa explained.

"They had to be the same Imperials the Wanderer told us about," Lisa said. "I bet they're after the Black Files, too. Or, they're after Bunker One."

"So they used us long enough to get the door open?" Makara asked.

"Yeah," Lisa said. "It's still hundreds of miles to Bunker One, though. They're probably heading for the motor pool."

"Did anyone catch where that was on the map?" I asked.

"I'm just concerned with getting out of here for now," Samuel said. "That means getting to the surface."

"*If* we can make it back to the surface," I said.

"We will," Samuel said. "I want to teach them a lesson they won't ever forget."

"A bullet in the head will make them forget pretty damn quickly," Makara said.

The corridor ended in another stairwell, spiraling upward. It led to a hatch. Samuel unlatched the door, and pushed it out. We found ourselves in a circular, vertical tunnel. A giant ladder crawled up the side into the darkness above.

"Nowhere to go but up," Makara said.

"What is it with Bunkers and really tall ladders?" I asked.

No one answered as Samuel took the lead. Over the next couple minutes, we climbed a hundred or so rungs. I tried not to look down. Looking down was like staring into an abyss. It was so dark that I couldn't tell how high we had climbed.

At last, the group came to a stop. Samuel struggled with the latch wheel at the top – I heard it squeak as he turned it. With a grunt, he forced the hatch open with his powerful shoulders.

Above, the cold wind howled.

We were going back outside.

I was the last one to crawl out of Bunker 40. As I stepped into the cold wind and slammed the hatch shut behind me, the squish of the xenofungus below my boots was not exactly a welcome change.

It was evening, and the skyscraper to the south was blazoned orange by the sunset. Unearthly screams and howls emanated from the distance. The monsters surrounded the building, thinking we were still there. I didn't want to stick around to find out how long it would take for them to figure out we weren't.

We had nothing but the clothes on our backs, our weapons, and the copious amounts of ammunition we had grabbed in the Officers' armory. Our Recon and supplies were back at the building, surrounded by monsters that we could never hope to break through.

Our choices were fighting our way through, or going on.

"What now?" I asked.

My voice sounded more hopeless than I'd intended. As the others talked about what to do next, Anna stood next to me and grabbed my hand. One by one, her fingers intertwined with mine.

I was shocked more than anything, because the move seemed to have come out of nowhere. I looked at her questioningly, but she remained silent.

"We'll find a way," she said. "Just don't give up."

What was left of the sun descended behind the western mountains, plunging the valley into darkness.

Anna let go of my hand as the others turned around.

"What did you guys decide?" Anna asked.

Samuel said nothing, merely shining his light down on the xenofungus. The layer here was thin, and beneath it was tarmac.

"A runway?" Makara asked.

"Yeah," Samuel said. "If there's a runway here, that hangar should be somewhere nearby. We'll die if we have to stay out here for the night."

"I don't see anything resembling a hangar out here," Lisa said.

"We'll just have to follow the runway and look," Samuel said.

"What about the Recon?" I asked.

"One thing at a time," Samuel said. "I just need to make sure we don't die from crawlers."

Something caught my eye. A vertical sliver of light appeared in the direction of a nearby hill.

"I think we found our hangar," I said.

The sliver grew wider and wider, revealing more light.

"It's built into that hill," Samuel said. "I think we found our friends."

The opening of the hangar was accompanied by a sound – the loud hum of an engine.

"Are they flying a plane?" I asked.

"I don't care," Makara said. "It's payback time."

Everyone ran ahead, and it was all I could do to keep up. As we got closer to the light, I could make out the shape of a low, sleek jet. As it rolled out of the hill and into the valley, the roar of its engine grew ever louder. That sound would draw every one of those creatures in this direction.

The plane took on a sudden burst of speed. It rocketed toward us, quickly closing the distance.

"Out of the way!" Samuel yelled.

Everyone dove out of the plane's way as it screamed past. I turned to watch its six thrusters, arranged in the shape of a circle, burn a fiery blue as the plane arched up from the ground and streaked through the sky. The plane's sound waves thundered against the ground as it disappeared into the night.

When the noise died, it was replaced with another one – the monsters, screeching and wailing.

"Let's move!" Samuel yelled.

Samuel sprinted for the open doors of the hangar. Behind, the creatures' unearthly screams came closer.

We entered the hangar doors. We had to find a way to close them before it was too late.

"Search for a switch," Samuel said. "Anything!"

My eyes scanned the walls. These doors had to close, or we'd be overwhelmed. I saw a silver box affixed to the wall. I opened the box and saw the words "Hangar Doors" above one of the many red buttons. I pressed it.

The doors screeched, forcing themselves shut ever so slowly.

I ran back to the front, where the rest of the group stood. Lisa had taken a position on top of some nearby crates, and was readying the scope of her rifle. Anna stood with her katana in front of her, as calm as if she were doing one of her practice routines. Makara held her pistol with both hands, facing outward. Samuel and I took our positions beside her, pointing our guns into the darkness.

A large, lumbering creature that might have once been a bear charged between the closing doors, going right for Makara. We unloaded into it, and it gave out a baleful roar as it snapped its jaws. With a long, fleshy arm, it began a swipe of its scythe-like claws at Makara. But a loud crack sounded in the hangar and the beast fell dead. Lisa had shot it in the head.

The doors were almost shut, but before they closed two more crawlers slipped in. They slithered along the ground with their bowed legs. Long, curved teeth lined the insides of their powerful jaws, and their all-white eyes burned fiercely.

They circled around us, waiting to strike. We fired at

them, but it was as if they could anticipate our movements. At every shot, they danced out of the way.

Lisa, from above, aimed at one of them, and bided her time for the perfect shot.

One of them broke, going straight for me. Anna stepped in front, using her blade as a shield. The creature screamed as its neck was ripped open by the blade, and purple liquid oozed from the gash. The crawler crumpled to the floor.

The other one hissed and fell upon Samuel like lightning. He was tackled to the floor, but before the creature could sink its teeth into his neck, Makara and I pulled it off. The crawler slipped from my hands, targeting me.

The creature collapsed on top of my chest, knocking the wind out of my lungs. Anna had shot it with her sidearm.

The others pulled the monster off me. It took a moment before I could breathe.

"You okay?" Makara asked.

I nodded weakly. "Yeah."

Everyone stood for a moment, catching their breaths. Outside, we could hear the horde screaming and howling.

"We need to secure the perimeter," Samuel said.

We walked around the large hangar, checking for any doors, holes, or cracks where anything could slip through. There seemed to be no entry except for where we had come in. Soon, I found myself focusing on the cargo plane that was still parked in the far corner of the hangar.

If they could fly a plane, who was to say we couldn't?

"I want to check that plane out," I said.

"Good idea," Samuel said. "There could be food, water, or other supplies. Why don't you and Anna do that?"

Anna nodded toward the plane. "Come on."

A boarding staircase led up to the door. I was afraid it might be locked, but the door opened right up when I tried the latch, revealing the plane's interior. Anna stepped inside, pointing her flashlight left and right. In the back of the plane were crates of MREs. Looking at the dates, though, I saw they were long expired.

We walked into the cockpit, where there were two large pilot chairs, and behind each of them were two additional seats. There were hundreds of buttons, a control stick in front of the pilot's chair, and a large LCD screen set in the control panel, midway between the pilot's and the copilot's chairs.

I was startled when the LCD screen flashed on automatically, as if detecting my presence. The screen displayed a map of the United States and was pinpointed with several red circles, each marked with a number – 21, 33, 105. I saw 108, right there in the San Bernardino Mountains. And, 114 was not too far northwest of it. These were Bunker locations.

I searched for 40. I found it in northeastern Arizona, near the border of New Mexico.

"Do you think this plane works?" Anna asked.

"It did for them," I said. "But maybe Harland is a trained pilot. None of us could ever fly this thing."

If we could, though, this plane would cut an enormous amount of time off our journey. We might even make it to Bunker One *tonight,* if only we had someone who knew how to fly.

I turned my attention back to the screen. Most of the numbering was gray. Bunkers 23, 40, 76, 88, 108, 114 had red lettering. I guessed that the gray meant that the bunker was no longer operational. At the time 40 had fallen, which must not have been too long ago, there were still six bunkers left. The only ones unaccounted for were 76 and 88. They were both located on the West

Coast – one near San Francisco, and the other near Portland. Not far enough for the Blights to have reached them. I wondered if they were still operating.

My attention homed in on Bunker One. There it was, right there: Cheyenne Mountain, Colorado. According to the map, we were at the halfway point.

I touched the red dot of Bunker One. The screen responded, and flashed.

"Location selected," came a female voice from the dash. "Initiating launch sequence."

"Oh, shit."

I searched madly for some way to abort it. But the screen had faded, and I could feel the plane thrum as the engines roared to life.

Samuel burst into the cockpit.

"Alex, what the hell is going on?"

I turned around. "I don't know. I just touched the screen and it turned the plane on."

Samuel scanned the screen. It had come back on, showing the map again. On top of the screen, it read, "autopilot engaged."

"Autopilot," Samuel said. "They weren't flying it at all. The plane's computer was doing it for them!"

"Is that where they're going?" I asked. "Bunker One?"

Everyone else ran into the cockpit.

"Alex, what the hell did you do?" Makara asked.

"I don't know, I..."

"Wait," Lisa said. "This might be our ticket out. We have no other chance with those monsters out there."

That was when the plane started moving. Everyone rocked forward, grabbing on the walls to keep from falling.

"The hangar doors!" Samuel said. "We can't leave if someone doesn't open them."

"Whoever does that might die," Makara said. "They

wouldn't be able to get back on the plane."

The plane started moving.

"Well," Samuel said. "We're screwed."

The plane wheeled toward the doors and stopped before them. Slowly, they rolled back on their own.

"They're opening!" Samuel said.

"Must have been programmed into the hangar," I said.

As soon as the doors opened even a crack, the monsters started pouring in. They could do nothing as the plane wheeled forward, crushing them beneath the front wheels.

"We can't take off as long as any of them are blocking the runway," Samuel said.

The plane's landing lights flashed on, revealing a sea of crawlers, their white glowing eyes staring back at us from the darkness. They pushed toward the plane as if of one mind.

"We're not going to make it," Makara said.

As soon as she said that, the plane stopped. In the back, I could hear something moving.

"What's going on?" I asked.

The plane seemed to pause for a moment, and then, the engines roared. We were pushed to the deck as the floor lifted up from under us.

"Find a chair and strap in," Samuel said. "We're taking off!"

I found the seat behind the copilot's chair and strapped myself in. As everyone else found their own seats, the plane paused, hovering in midair. I could hear the thrusters turning again and engaging, and we surged forward. The acceleration pushed me back into my seat.

We arced upward toward the night sky, leaving the Great Blight under us. I looked out the window to see the glowing surface fading away.

EIGHTEEN

W e had been on the plane an hour when I headed back into the cargo area. I found a seat where I could get a moment of quiet before the plane descended.

Next to me was a circular window, and I could not stop looking out of it. For the first time in my life, I saw the moon and stars.

They sparkled in their thousands, dotting the midnight sky. I never imagined there would be so many. Though beautiful, they made me feel sad, in a way. We had lost so much because of Ragnarok. It would take decades, maybe even centuries, for the fallout to dissipate enough for them to be seen from the surface. How many generations would that take? Would there even be another generation to watch them?

"You look quite pensive."

It was Anna. She took the seat next to me, waiting for me to respond.

"I've never seen the night sky before," I said.

Anna looked out the window with me. "Neither have I. It's beautiful, isn't it?"

I nodded, but didn't say anything else.

"Look," she said. "Sorry if that was weird, earlier."

It took me a moment to realize she was talking about holding my hand.

"Don't worry about it," I said. "I've just been wondering...what made you do it?"

It took her a moment to answer. "I don't know. I guess...oh, it doesn't matter. Sometimes I don't understand why I do things."

I smiled. "Are you flustered?"

"Oh, quiet. Let's just forget it." Before I could say anything, she quickly changed the subject. "I almost wish we didn't have to go back down. The stars are better company than those monsters."

"We have to do what we have to do," I said. "This is our mission, and we'll see it through to the end. I just hope this plane can land as well as it takes off."

"I guess we'll find out soon, huh?"

"Guess so."

"Anna, I just wanted to say...I'm glad you stayed."

"You're sweet," she said. "But my reasons are my own. You guys need me, and like the Wanderer said...my part isn't over, yet."

"Do you think we'll make it back alive?"

Anna paused as she considered. "I don't know anything more than you. The only thing we can do is complete each task that's put before us. When taken together, it seems too much, but tackling goals one at a time is the way you get from Point A to Point Z. Let's just focus on getting to Bunker One before we focus on saving the world."

She had a point, there. Before I could say anything else, my stomach lifted as the plane began its descent.

"We're already there?" I asked.

"It's not a long flight," Anna said. "Planes go incredibly fast. I never thought I'd ever fly in one." She moved to stand. "We should probably head up front."

We both stood, but some turbulence rocked the plane, sending us both to the deck. The plane rocked for the next few seconds before it steadied. Once it had cleared, we went to the cockpit and strapped ourselves into the two open seats, readying ourselves for what could be a rough landing.

WE ENTERED THE LAYER OF RED CLOUDS, AND THE STARS above were lost for good. I probably would never see them again.

The LCD map showed us to be almost directly above Bunker One. The clouds soon broke, revealing a large mountain covered with snow and dead trees. The plane approached quickly, seeming not to avert its course.

Samuel grabbed the control stick and tried forcing it left. But it was completely locked in place.

We were going to crash.

"Wait," Anna said, pointing. "I see something."

There was a straight line built into the mountainside. A landing strip was built into the side of the mountain.

"It's taking us there," I said. "It was right all along."

Samuel let go of the control stick. The plane veered to the right toward the runway.

"Looks like they're already here," Samuel said, pointing to the plane parked at the runway's end.

"I wonder if they know we followed," I said. "Did they go to Bunker 40 because they knew about the planes?"

"Maybe," Lisa said.

The long runway stretched out before us. I could hear the plane's wheels deploy from the bottom of the hull. We descended toward the mountainside.

That was when I saw that the runway was not completely empty.

A few crawlers covered the runway. We landed with a thud, the wheels skidding on the tarmac.

The brakes automatically slowed the plane, but from time to time, a crawler crunched under the wheel, rocking the plane and throwing it off-kilter.

The edge of the runway was fast approaching, and there was nothing but darkness beyond. We were slowing – but it wouldn't be enough.

"We need to jump out," Samuel said. "Come on!"

We got up and struggled our way to the door. Samuel reached it first, unlatched it, and pushed it open. Below the plane, the tarmac glided by. We were still going too fast.

A moment later, the plane had slowed enough to allow a jump. Makara was the first to go, tucking in and landing with a roll. Anna followed after her, then Lisa.

Samuel nodded. "Go, Alex!"

I jumped, feeling the cold wind rush past my face and butterflies rise in my stomach. God, this was going to hurt. I landed with a thud, tucking in like Makara, rolling forward to break my fall. A moment later, I had skidded to a stop.

I stood, finding myself at the edge of the runway, mere feet from the cliff. I saw Samuel on my right roll to a stop. He cried out in pain, probably from hurting his arm.

With a thunderous creak on my left, the plane tilted forward and slid down the mountainside. The giant vehicle crashed into the rocks below, sending up an enormous plume of flame. The reek of jet fuel stung my nostrils and lungs as the fire heated my face with its glow.

Makara went to help Samuel up. "You all right?"

"Fine," he said. "The pain should subside soon."

"We need to get inside," Anna said, stepping forward. "Those crawlers are coming."

There was an open door built into the mountainside – the entrance to Bunker One. In their haste, Harland and Drake must have left it open.

"We have to reach the Black Files before they do," Makara said.

"We know this place like the back of our hands," Samuel said. "We just have to get to the research lab and the Files."

Anna drew her blade. "We have company."

Three of the crawlers loped toward our position. Their long necks and heads undulated back and forth, and jagged teeth jutted from their mouths. Their white eyes blazed in the dark night.

The first crawler charged for Makara, letting out a high screech. Anticipating its move, she dodged to the side in a fluid motion, arching back her knife to deliver a killing blow in its neck. The monster squealed as purple goo sprayed from the wound, convulsing before growing still.

Anna charged for the other two. They broke, surrounding her on both sides. I ran forward, Beretta in hand, firing at the one on the left and scoring a few shots. It hissed before charging after me.

Samuel stepped beside me, and together, we fired at it. With a shriek, the crawler fell dead, its momentum carrying it forward before it stopped at our feet.

Anna handled the last one with an expert swing of her blade, severing its head from its body.

"That takes care of that," she said.

"Inside!" Samuel said.

We ran for Bunker One across the tarmac, the cold wind tearing at my skin. It must have been way below freezing in the frigid mountain air.

We stepped inside the Bunker and slammed the metal door shut behind us. Samuel latched it, and a few seconds later the creatures that had been chasing us slammed against the door.

"I can't believe it," Makara said. "We're actually here."

Someone had left the lights on. Before us was a long hallway with no doors on either side.

"This tunnel goes on for a while," Makara said. "It leads to some stairs and a bank of elevators."

"Is this the only way to the runway?" I asked.

"There's a large hangar, but this is the way Samuel and I came when we escaped. More of a side entrance." She paused. "Ten thousand people used to live here, and only a handful survived that night."

Her eyes were distant. I knew what she was thinking – her parents might be in here, somewhere, but if they were, they were probably no longer human.

"We have to go," Samuel said. "Get the Files, and bury the past once and for all."

Samuel headed forward, into the tunnel. We followed.

NINETEEN

M akara was right; Bunker One was huge.
We made it to the elevator bank, then
continued on to the stairwell and descended...down
and down and down. I stopped counting after twenty
flights.

"There are fifty-two floors," Makara said. "Not
counting the L-Levels."

"L-Levels?" I asked.

"The labs," she said. "Only scientists were allowed
in. It is protected by a huge vault door, not unlike the
ones that guard a normal Bunker from the outside. They
didn't want anyone getting in that wasn't supposed to
be there."

"I wonder what they were hiding," I said.

"That's what we're here to find out," Samuel said.
"You have no idea how long I've waited for this
moment."

"It's too quiet," Anna said. "I don't like it."

"Yeah," Lisa said. "Would have expected something
to be attacking us in here. But it's like someone came in
and cleaned everything up."

"The lights are on, too," Anna said. "Someone's keeping house."

"Harland and Drake, maybe," I said.

We fell into silence, and it wasn't long before we'd arrived at the first floor.

"Be careful," Samuel said. "If they know we followed, they'll be setting another trap."

Samuel forced the door open, and my breath caught. "Giant" did not even begin to describe the room we had entered. No, not a room. A chamber, a cavern, though manmade. It must have taken years to carve out.

It was basically a gigantic vertical tunnel, like the interior of a silo. I looked up and saw the rock ceiling hundreds of feet above. It probably would take at least a minute to walk across the chamber's entire diameter. The railed edges of floor upon floor ringed the tunnel's circumference. It was like a circular skyscraper, only underground. Lights lit the place only dimly, so I couldn't see its entire scope. Hundreds of doors and openings and archways lined the floors – things that looked as if they had once been stores, services, restaurants, apartments, or places to relax.

This hadn't been a Bunker. It had been an entire underground city. Everyone besides Makara and Samuel stared for a moment in wonder.

In front of us was a red stain on the rock floor, the remains of someone's grisly death years before. The body was gone.

"Labs are this way," Samuel said.

We followed Samuel across the massive chamber, but I couldn't keep from looking up. It must have taken an army of thousands of monsters to bring down a place like this.

Samuel went through a large opening and into a wide corridor. The corridor sloped downward. The echoes of our footsteps were loud. Anyone or anything would hear us coming from a mile away.

A bullet whizzed past my head, forcing me to the ground. Everyone else followed suit.

"They're right ahead of us," Samuel said.

I looked ahead. Both Harland and Drake were kneeling behind a railing that served as a barricade. They were right in front of the vault door. More bullets were fired.

"Damn it, there's no cover!" Samuel said.

"If they want me to open it again, they're out of luck," I said.

"I don't think anyone could open that, other than with brute force," Samuel said.

"Well," Makara said, "let's take care of these guys, first."

"Wait," I said. "Something's wrong."

Harland and Drake had ceased their fire. It was as if they were trying to see what we were going to do.

That was when an explosion rocked the entire tunnel. It shook the ceiling, the walls, and the floor. Rock cracked and fell from above, threatening to bury us alive.

We scrambled up and ran forward under a hail of bullets. They were forcing us out of the tunnel and right into their sights.

A bullet nicked my boot, but luckily, it didn't hit anything. But a few more seconds of this and all of us would be dead.

I fell to the ground behind a large rock that had crashed against the floor. Everyone else took their places beside me as the tunnel behind continued to collapse on itself.

I looked into the dark tunnel we had just run out of, but rocks had buried the entire thing. That was when I noticed Lisa was missing.

"Lisa?" Makara shouted.

The last of the rocks fell into the tunnel, leaving only a small space to crawl out of. Nothing else moved.

Makara shook her head. *"Lisa!"*

Samuel grabbed her shoulder. "Don't."

"She's gone," I said.

"We have to stay alive," Samuel said. "We can't get out of cover."

Even if we got out of this one alive, we were stuck. The tunnel behind had collapsed, and Harland and Drake were guarding the door.

Makara reached into her pack. Tears in her eyes, she held a grenade.

"This might work," she said. "As soon as it goes off, we'll charge the bastards and finish the job."

No one said anything as she pulled the plug, waited a second, and lobbed it overhand. She closed her eyes, waiting for the boom.

Nothing happened. It was a dud.

No one said anything. It was as if everyone had given up.

"Nice try," Harland said. "Just open the door, like last time. If you do, we'll spare your lives."

"I'm not opening that damn thing for you," I yelled. "You just killed one of our own."

"Those Black Files are ours," Harland said. "This is the sovereign territory of the Empire, and anything in it belongs to us."

"You'll have to kill us first," I said.

"We're working on that," Harland said. "Serves you right for Kris earlier."

"That was no one's fault, and you damn well know it," Samuel said.

Harland didn't respond, and it was another moment before he spoke.

"It seems we have reached an impasse. One of us is

going to have to back down. Those Black Files are not going to be yours."

"We need them," Samuel said. "With that info we can find out how to stop the Blights. Maybe even the xenovirus. You have no idea what you're doing by taking those files back to the Empire."

"I don't understand," Anna said. "Aren't the files digital? Why can't we both have them?"

"The Empire doesn't want anyone else to have that info," Harland said.

"Well, you can't get in there unless we open the door," I said. "You need us, and you're not getting anywhere without us. And guess what? We're not helping you."

"I'm tired of this," Makara said. "They die now."

"No," I said. "You'll get yourself killed."

Makara sighed. "I don't care. Someone has to attack them. There's four of us and two of them. No one's getting out of here alive, so we have to make a move at some point."

A loud shot rang out in the room. It came from the rubble in the tunnel. I heard Drake scream from behind the barricade.

"Lisa," I said. "She's alive!"

Another shot fired. It zinged off the metal. I heard Harland curse from the direction of the door.

"Now!" Samuel said.

We all followed Samuel's lead as he emerged from behind the boulder and charged for the door. Harland was still in shock at being sniped at, so he didn't react fast enough. As he was raising his gun, Samuel, Makara, and I all shot him. He gave a raspy groan as his eyes widened. He fell to his knees, right beside Drake, who had a bullet in his forehead.

We turned around, but Lisa was not in sight. It was

only as we ran back to the pile of rubble that we found her.

She was lying on the ground in a pool of her own blood. A sharp rock had gashed into her neck from above, where blood was slowly leaking out – but judging from the amount on the floor, it didn't look as if there was much left.

Anna dug into her pack for a first aid kit.

"I don't have long," Lisa said. "Don't even bother."

"Lisa!" Makara said. "Lisa, you hear me?"

"Yeah. I'm here."

Lisa's face was pale, and her blue eyes were barely open. Still, she held her rifle.

"Lisa..."

Samuel took a shirt from his pack and placed it on a nasty gash on Lisa's neck. She hissed in pain as pressure was applied. Too much blood was still pouring out.

"I said, don't." she said. "The old man was right."

"What do you mean?" Makara asked, tears coming to her eyes.

Lisa gave a weak smile. "He said I didn't have long, but without me..." She coughed, blood sputtering from her mouth.

"No," Makara said. "You still have to try. You can't give up."

"Take my gun," she said. "Don't leave it here, in this place."

Makara shook her head again. "No. You're not going to die. Quit saying that."

"The old man was right. I did my part..."

"Lisa..."

Lisa's hauntingly blue eyes stared upward, and she never completed her sentence. She relaxed against the hard ground, her wavy brown hair fanned and matted to the floor from her blood.

Makara's shoulders shook. Her face was a mixture of

anger and devastation. She still held Lisa's lifeless hand. It looked as if she would never let it go.

No one said a word. I just stared at Lisa, tears coming to my eyes.

Finally, Makara stood, her face hardening. She grabbed the sniper rifle, and threw it over her back by the strap.

"Makara."

She turned to face me. Her face was harder than the rock of the walls. She didn't say anything. Already, her tears had dried.

"Let's go," she said. "We're wasting time."

No one moved as Makara knelt down to shut Lisa's eyes, her hand shaking.

"I'm sorry," she said.

Makara stood again, and we watched as she walked to the vault door. She ignored the bodies of Harland and Drake, not even minding their blood. Her boots made a sticky sound as she stood before the door.

"This is Makara Neth, citizen of Bunker One. Open the door."

The doors did not respond. Makara stood, her arms flexing. The door stayed shut, immovable as a mountain.

"It's no good," Samuel said. "We don't have clearance. None of us do."

Makara pounded on the door. "Cornelius Ashton...I know you're in there. I know you didn't die. You need to open this door. *Now.*"

Anna and I looked at each other. Cornelius Ashton, author of the Black Files...*was* he still alive?

"Cornelius?" Anna whispered.

"Dr. Cornelius Ashton," I said. "But he's dead. He's not here..."

"Someone's here," Samuel said. "Someone has the lights on. Someone cleaned up all the bodies."

Makara was screaming. "Open this goddamn door!"

The vault door hissed, creaking open inch by inch. The lab within was dark. Makara continued standing in front of the door.

She turned to us. "Come on."

She walked into the darkness of the labs. We rushed to join her.

Lisa's body was still. It seemed so wrong to leave her here, but we had no other choice.

The Black Files awaited us.

TWENTY

We entered the main part of the lab. Hundreds of computers, powered off, sat in long lines in the middle of the room. Chairs still sat in front of most of them. Unlike the rest of the bunker, this part was clean.

Against the far wall was a large screen. As soon as we entered the room the fluorescent lights powered on, temporarily blinding me. The computers in their long lines snapped on one by one, filling the room with an iridescent glow. Large machines against the walls – probably more computers – powered on with low hums. The entire lab was starting up. I wondered where the power source was, and how it was still running after all these years.

Samuel walked to the big screen, and stood at a terminal before it.

There was no sign of Dr. Ashton. The lab looked as empty as it probably had been for the past twelve years.

But if that was so, then who opened the door? And for that matter, who had opened the door at Bunker 40?

"He's not here," I said.

"It doesn't matter," Samuel said. "The Files are ours."

The computer was already on, ready to go. All Samuel had to do was do a search for the Black Files. We would have them in seconds.

Samuel typed "Black Files" into the computer's search bar. Instantly, a link appeared: *Black Files, The. Dr. Cornelius Ashton. Compiled Xenobiological Research, 2042-2048, property of the Government of the United States of America. CLASSIFIED. Security Clearance Omega.*

"Security Clearance Omega?" I asked.

"It means the U.S. does not want us accessing these files," Samuel said. "But I'll try."

Makara watched, not speaking. Anna stood nearby with katana in hand.

"I'll try my own login credentials from Bunker 114. Maybe that will be good enough."

Samuel logged in, and a message flashed across the screen: *Access granted. Welcome, Assistant Chief Scientist, Samuel Neth.*

"Assistant Chief Scientist," Anna said. "Sounds serious."

"That was not my station," Samuel said. "Someone's updated this to recognize my name."

"Congrats on your promotion," I said.

Makara remained silent, her face like stone.

They were on the screen: the Black Files we'd all been waiting for.

"The summary is only eighty pages long," Samuel said, with a frown. "I was expecting more. Much more."

"You sound disappointed," I said.

Samuel shrugged. "Just not what I expected at all. Then again, a lot can sometimes be said with a little, but that's typically not the case with research papers."

"Read it," Anna said. "This is what we're here for. Let's see how to beat this thing."

Samuel sighed. "All right. Reading."

Samuel scanned the pages furiously. He showed no reaction as we waited. Occasionally, he mouthed something to himself. At the end of ten minutes his face darkened.

"What is it?" I asked.

Samuel held up a hand. As he read, his expression became more and more disturbed.

"What's going on?" Anna asked.

"Did you finish?" I asked.

Samuel nodded. "Yeah. You're not going to believe where the xenovirus came from. Well, maybe you will, because I suspected it all along. But you will definitely not know *why* it's here."

"Well," Makara said. "We have time. Tell us what you found out."

———

"As I suspected," Samuel said, "the xenovirus is not of Earth origin. Looking at the flora and fauna it creates should be enough indication of that."

"It was inside Ragnarok, wasn't it?" I asked.

Samuel nodded. "Yes. That's the only way it could have come. In the Old World, NASA did experiments on how long bacteria and viruses could last in the vacuum of space. In some cases, it might be years or longer. The xenovirus was lodged in Ragnarok, and the rock protected it from the cold vacuum of space. That's not all, though."

"What else?"

Samuel sighed. "A lot."

He paused a moment, as if collecting his thoughts. I had a feeling we were about to get a huge dose of information.

"Are you familiar with the Guardian Missions?"

Samuel asked.

It sounded familiar, but it was a moment before the memory returned to me.

"There were three," I said. "They were the world's attempt to stop Ragnarok from destroying Earth. All of them failed."

"That's right," Samuel said. "Each Guardian Mission had a name, also the name of the ship launched. The first, called the *Archangel*, was launched in 2024. It reached Ragnarok after a flight of six months. The story is that something went wrong with the landing gear, which caused the ship to crash."

"Okay," I said. "So what really happened?"

"There's only a few paragraphs of it in here," Samuel said. "But apparently it was something else. The ship landed fine. They were even able to install the rockets on the surface of Ragnarok, which was the original plan for pushing it off course. But they were attacked."

We looked at each other.

"Wait," Makara said. "I can understand viruses and microbes surviving. But attacked? Anything capable of harming a person couldn't withstand space. It's impossible."

"Whatever it was, it wasn't built like we are. There are pictures, even. One of the astronauts managed to get a photo but it didn't turn out well. You can only see a worm-like creature."

We crowded around the computer. Indeed, there was a picture of something, probably living.

"Creepy," Makara said.

"Looks like a crawler," I said. "The shot is blurry."

"Information about the attack was held back in order to prevent panic. Another mission was planned, with more people. This one was called *Reckoning*."

"I always did think that name sounded funny," I said.

"They sent soldiers with this one, along with the crew. They had guns. Only this mission never made it to the asteroid in the first place. The story was that it got lost on the way there, and that one appears to be true if what I read here is correct. Perhaps hit by a stray piece of rock or debris, or something wrong with the engine or hull."

"No reckoning, then."

"No," Samuel said. "There was the last mission in 2028. The one that appeared to succeed, but didn't. The *Messiah* mission."

We all waited for Samuel to go on.

"*Messiah* made it to Ragnarok and landed without a hitch. The rockets were attached to Ragnarok. Like the *Archangel* mission, it seemed to work. When the crawlers or whatever they were came, they were driven back. Eventually, the astronauts were overwhelmed – but not before the rockets began to go off, doing their job in pushing Ragnarok off course."

"Why didn't it work?"

"Because the rockets needed a full week to do their job effectively. The astronauts did all they could – but they fell, one by one, to endless waves of attackers. Whatever was on the asteroid, it had planned on being able to defend it."

"Defend it?" Anna asked. "Why? Did it want to attack us?"

Samuel nodded. "Yes. After this mission failed, the government said that they had thought the mission was a success, but for reasons unknown, it didn't work. From the Files, we know why. Ragnarok was pushed off course, but not by much. Not by enough."

A horrible dread twisted my gut. I knew all this happened thirty years ago, but it was hard not to imagine how everyone must have felt as these missions failed, one by one.

"The Bunker Program began immediately in 2020, shortly after Ragnarok's discovery. This was the beginning of what came to be known as the Dark Decade. Ragnarok was to hit Earth on December 3, 2030 – Dark Day. The Bunkers were never meant to be a reality. They were supposed to be Plan B. The government believed that if Ragnarok impacted Earth, they needed enough people underground to come up and rebuild once it was all over. The key to this was making well-trained soldiers of all underground U.S. citizens. The Bunkers altogether, assuming no losses, had enough space to hold close to 60,000 people. Given they were all well-trained, that's still a sizable force for an army. But as we all know, that wasn't to last. The world became much darker than anyone expected. Things broke down. As far as we know, there are only two Bunkers. Maybe even they are gone by now."

"How come Ragnarok took so long to detect?" I asked. "You'd think they would have found it much earlier than they did."

"In the Old World, NASA funded the NEO Program – the Near Earth Object Program, designed to do just that. Asteroids the size of Ragnarok or larger were all accounted for, but Ragnarok went rogue, somehow. It changed course in what seemed to be an impossible manner. No one knows exactly *when* this occurred, but it took a while before people noticed. To this day, no one knows how it was done. But we know *why* it was done."

"Why?" I asked, dreading the answer. "Why did it change course?"

"The answer is simple. We're being invaded."

TWENTY-ONE

"Nothing else explains the attacks on Ragnarok's surface while it was still in space," Samuel continued, "or how something the size of Ragnarok could suddenly change course like it did."

"Maybe something else hit it," I said. "Another asteroid. It's possible, right? It could have been hit and been put on a course to hit Earth."

"The odds of that are so small that the alien scenario seems much more likely. Given enough energy, Ragnarok's course could have been switched. It's mind-bending mathematically, but maybe they could do it."

"And who are *they*?" Makara asked. "Those creatures that have been attacking us? Because they don't seem to be that smart. Their strength is in numbers."

"I don't know everything, and the Black Files don't speak to that. But there does seem to be *something* that demonstrates intelligence, something referred to in the Files only as 'The Voice.'"

"'The Voice?'" Makara asked. "Are you kidding me?"

Samuel shook his head. "This is the meat of the Black

Files. Everything I explained was only the first twenty pages. The rest of it is about this – the xenovirus, the xenofungus, and the Voice. And a day in the future called Xenofall."

"Xenofall?" Makara asked.

"Explanation, please," Anna said.

"Let me start at the beginning," Samuel said. "Ragnarok hit in 2030, as you all know. Almost immediately the virus took effect. The first instances were noted as early as 2031, in Bunker 23 out in western Nebraska. It was the Bunker closest to Ragnarok, and it was the first to go offline in 2034."

"It wouldn't be long until others went offline, too," I said.

"That's true," Samuel said. "And most Bunkers failed for reasons having nothing to do with the xenovirus. Interestingly, the xenovirus's main job is not to infect life-forms on Earth. It's to create xenofungus."

"Why?" I asked.

"It's the food source for all xenolife," Samuel said. "Yeah, xenolife will eat animals, or even people, from time to time. There are nutrients there. But even I noticed in my research that xenofungus is nutrient and calorie heavy. It is death and poison to any of us, but it sustains anything infected with the xenovirus. It could be that the xenovirus is as much an enzyme as it is a virus, an enzyme that can process the fungus and make it edible."

"So the xenofungus is like alien farms, or something?" Anna asked.

"Yes. That's a good way to think of it." Samuel paused. "It also does other stuff. It reproduces rapidly, and can survive in very harsh environments. It doesn't need much water. It doesn't mind the cold, or the dryness. It's as if it's been engineered to survive almost any sort of environment, and *especially* environments without much sunlight. It's perfectly adapted for surviving in a world that is cloaked from sunlight by meteor fallout, which explains how it is able to spread so easily while everything of Earth origin dies off. We're in the process of being transformed from Earth into something that's *not* Earth."

"What about the monsters?" I asked. "How does the xenovirus do that?"

"It's all encoded in the xenovirus's DNA," Samuel said. "It does not have a double helix, like Earth-based life. It's a very complicated cloverleaf structure, something that is very hard to imagine evolving in the wild – at least on Earth. This might be evidence pointing to the xenovirus being designed. The cloverleaf lends certain advantages. It can hold more information. It's more adaptable. It has the capability to plug in genes of Earth creatures, creating entirely new forms of life, such as the crawlers. The xenovirus was probably created."

"Created by whom?" I asked.

Samuel shook his head. "We couldn't have done this. We don't have the technology. It must have been created by an alien intelligence."

"So you're saying the xenovirus was *planted* in Ragnarok?"

"Exactly," Samuel said.

"What about this Voice thing?" Makara asked. "You didn't explain that."

"It's like a sentience for all life forms infected with the virus. It's all based on the fungus, somehow. The fungus, in addition to being food, is also like a giant neural network. Fungus in one part of the world, as long as it is connected, can communicate with fungus in another part. It's like a giant brain that can think – and yes, speak."

"Speak? How?"

"Most of it is internal and can't be heard. The

communication can't be deciphered by humans, much less translated in any way humans can understand. They were working on that, before Bunker One fell. Nonetheless, this communication takes place. It creates sound waves, language that directly affects the behavior of xenolife. During the attack on Bunker One, for example, the sound waves escalated as the Bunker began to be attacked. This Voice lends sentience to the entire invasion."

"Can it be killed?" I asked.

"You'd have to kill the xenofungus," Samuel said. "Whether the Voice is actually connected with a physical body, the Black Files don't say. I guess they didn't get that far."

"There is still so much we don't know," I said. "We don't even know if we can stop this."

"Yeah, that's the bottom line," Makara said. "Can we stop this? What's the next step?" She pointed outside the lab. "Because if you tell me Lisa came out here and died for nothing, we wasted a life."

"I honestly don't know," Samuel said. "If this sentience, this Voice, were somehow destroyed, I guess that could make all xenolife directionless. I don't know how we'd go about doing that."

"Great," Anna said. "This just gets more and more impossible."

No one said anything. It was a lot to take in. Even though we knew where it came from, even why it was here, we were no closer to knowing *how* to stop the xenovirus. Nothing definitive, anyway. Kill the Voice – but how do you kill something that isn't attached to a corporeal form?

I was expecting the answer to be obvious. I was expecting something like a chemical or a drug that would kill anything that had the xenovirus – an actual cure that targeted the xenovirus and eradicated it.

Knowing how something existed didn't tell you how to make it no longer exist.

"Do the Files say anything else?" I asked. "Anything at all on how to kill this thing?"

"No," Samuel said.

So, that was it. If these researchers couldn't figure anything out – in the Bunker with the biggest labs, the most computers, and most expertise – what shot did we have? We were only four. Other than pure guesswork, there was almost no hope.

Within a certain amount of time, the world would be covered with Blights. There would only be one Blight, and humanity would no longer exist.

"THERE'S ONE THING YOU DIDN'T EXPLAIN," MAKARA SAID.

Samuel looked up from where he had been hanging his head. His form was hunched in near defeat – it was disconcerting to see that in our leader.

"Explain what Xenofall is."

"Xenofall is what it sounds like," Samuel said. "The writers and moviemakers in the Old World always thought aliens would attack with giant ships and lasers. Nothing is further from reality. It's all biological warfare, and the most brilliant kind there is: the kind that weakens us, and empowers them."

"So when the meteor fell, it was only clearing the way," I said. "When the rest of them come, the natives will be gone, so to speak."

Samuel nodded. "Earth is being terraformed. Not by giant machines of metal, but by tiny machines of life. When they're through, Earth will not be ours anymore. We will have been long dead, and the planet will be ready for them to use. We're being colonized."

"When will this 'Xenofall' happen?" I asked.

"The Files don't say," Samuel said. "However long it takes for us to die out, and however long it takes for the Blights to cover the Earth. But we're the only ones who can stop it. That is, if it *can* be stopped."

Samuel walked from the computer. In that lab, with the hundreds of computers humming around us, Xenofall seemed like a date that would never happen. But it was real. It was coming. And we had no way of stopping it.

"We need more information," Samuel said. "But this..." He waved his arm around, indicating the entire room. "This is all there is. We know more than anyone else on Earth knows, but still, it's not enough."

"What more can we do?" I asked. "We're stuck here in the Bunker, surrounded by hundreds of miles of Blight and monsters, with winter coming on and no way out. And probably no food or water. Looks like we're as good as dead."

Samuel ignored my cheery assessment. "The only thing I can think of is going to Ragnarok Crater."

My insides lurched at the thought. We had just gotten here, of all places, and Samuel was talking about picking up and going to the Ragnarok Crater, another thousand miles away?

"You can't be serious," Makara said.

Samuel looked completely serious to me. "This is pure speculation, but it makes sense to think the Crater would be the center of it all. It's where the meteor landed and began its work. There might be some central hub where everything communicates with each other."

"Key words: *pure speculation*," Makara said. "We came here. We found nothing. We lose. We found our answer. The answer is: there is no answer. This was all for nothing. All we can do is hope to get out of here, find the safest place we can, and wait for the end."

"We're not getting out of here," I said. "Our ride blew itself up. It was a miracle that thing even flew."

Something quite unexpected happened. A voice came from every speaker in the lab, booming from the walls.

"Everyone," the voice said, "this is Dr. Cornelius Ashton. Do you read me?"

We stared at each other in shock. So he *was* here.

"Yes!" Samuel yelled. "Dr. Ashton, where are you?"

"I'm not in Bunker One," Dr. Ashton said, "but there is little time to explain. With luck, there will be time for that later. You all will die if you stay in this lab a minute longer."

"Die?" Anna asked. "What do you know? How are you even talking to us?"

"Never mind that. I'll explain later. All that matters is getting out of here alive. *It* knows you're here. The Voice. Every Blighter within a hundred-mile radius is converging on this point. It never *wanted* you to know what you have learned here today. Remember that the old axiom is true: information is power. And the Voice doesn't want you to have it.

"There will be time for answers soon, but now, you must escape this place. Already, they are inside."

As soon as those words were said, there was a crash against the vault door. I could hear the creatures' screams and wails coming from the other side.

"Get to the runway," Dr. Ashton said. "I'll provide your escape."

With that, the voice cut off. The silence that followed was pierced by more screams from infected creatures.

But they weren't just coming from the outside. Horrible cries sounded from deeper within the lab.

Howlers.

TWENTY-TWO

Howlers charged from two corridors leading into the main lab. Their clothes had long since rotted from their bodies, and what they had left were mere rags. They slunk toward us, flesh pink and thin, coated with purple slime.

"Don't shoot!" Samuel said. "Head for the stairs!"

We followed Samuel away from our attackers to the staircase that led to the lab's second level. I didn't know if there was a way out up there, but there sure wasn't one on the bottom floor. Both of the corridors had been blocked off.

We reached the landing and found no way out. The second floor was just a balcony that surrounded the entire lab.

"That door was the only way out," Makara said. "We're trapped."

"There has to be another way," I said. "Let's just keep looking."

Some of the Howlers charged for the stairs. We had to keep moving.

We followed Samuel around the balcony until we

had reached the other side. We were above the computers where we had searched for the Black Files – there were no doors, no windows, nor any other way back down to the lab floor. And now Howlers spilling from the balcony doorway cut us off on both sides.

"We're going to have to kill them," Anna said. "Explosions or not, we're dead either way."

"Kill these," Samuel said, pointing to the left. "We'll bring 'em down quick and jump off for the floor, and run deeper into the labs. I can see no other way."

We rushed to do just that. I aimed my Beretta, firing it into the oncoming Howlers. They shrieked as my bullets connected. I hit one creature in the head, and it crashed to the floor; the one behind stumbled over its body. In quick succession, Anna sliced one of the Howlers in half, and beheaded another. Makara fired, each shot finding its mark right in the head.

They were starting to swell, and would explode in moments.

"Now!" Samuel shouted.

We hopped over the railing, landing on top of a large computer. We jumped the rest of the way down. Though not as dangerous as the plane jump, the falls were a shock to my knees. I forced myself up, hoping I could run the pain out.

I hobbled after the others as they went to the empty corridor. Above us, the bodies popped and purple goo rained down, drenching the floor. We made it into the corridor.

A Howler emerged from a nearby door, his mouth agape and dripping slime. Quickly, Anna stabbed him through the heart, retrieved the blade, spun, and sliced off his head. She kicked the torso into the room from which the Howler had come.

"There has to be some other exit," Samuel said.

We followed the corridor at a near sprint. The

infected were falling further and further behind, but their howls still pierced the air. The hallway ended in a giant chamber filled with large machinery. It reminded me of the fusion reactor we had come across in Bunker 114. However, this chamber was much larger, though, which was saying a lot; that one had been big. Four reactors rose from the floor, the power source for all Bunker One. Only one was running – likely the only one that still worked.

"These things can run forever if maintained properly," Samuel said. "Or maybe not even maintained properly. It explains how this place still has power."

"This isn't time for a lesson, Samuel," Makara said. She pointed to a nearby ladder. "If we can reach the top catwalk, we might find a way to make it to the runway."

We ran for the ladder. We began our long climb. I felt dwarfed by the gigantic size of all the room's machinery

We had reached two-thirds of the way up when the chamber was filled with the echoes of hundreds of horrifying shrieks. I could not see where they were coming from, but looking up, I saw them.

Entering through the ceiling, through air ducts and hidden openings, came hundreds upon hundreds of birds. *Turned* birds. They swarmed for us like locusts, their white eyes glowing and their wings beating madly.

"Hurry it up, Samuel!" Makara yelled.

The swarm of birds homed in on our position. There were hundreds – big, small, but they all had one purpose – to kill us and keep us from reaching the top.

There was no way we could fight these. We had to get out of here.

Makara fired into the mass from the ladder, and a couple of the flying things plummeted toward the floor.

We reached the top and ran away from the avian swarm by making for a nearby door.

"Inside here," Samuel said.

We rushed in, finding ourselves in another corridor. Samuel slammed the door shut, locking it against the birds outside. They slammed into the door, pecking it, to no avail.

"Glad we got out of that one," Anna said.

"Yeah," I said. I turned forward, and after what I saw ahead, I almost wanted to try my luck with the birds.

BEFORE US STOOD A CREATURE AT LEAST TWENTY FEET TALL, with three heads on snakelike stalks, and a long, spiky tail – a creature that could only be described as a Hydra.

It was the most alien thing I'd ever seen, and each of its three mouths bore long, sharp teeth that dripped purple saliva. It walked on four muscular legs, and its scales were the color of crimson blood. Its necks stiffened, and the three heads opened their mouths to scream, each a different pitch, producing the most jarring, discordant noise I'd ever heard.

It charged forward lightning-fast. We didn't even have time to shoot before it slammed all four of us back into the door from which we'd come.

One of the heads was in front of me, snapping around my face. I dodged it, but I couldn't keep that up forever. When the head reared back on its stalk, I took the chance to grab the neck. I could feel the hard scales and the muscles bulging beneath. I slammed it with the butt of my Beretta. The thing screamed, hacking up purple phlegm that spewed onto the wall behind me.

The neck went still for a moment, so I aimed and fired.

It screamed again. I had hit it, but the shot had made no visible wound. Those scales were strong if bullets couldn't pierce them. All I had managed to do was piss it off.

Its head reared back again before shooting forward, nearly sinking its teeth into me. Instead, its face slammed against the door, making a dent in the metal.

I grabbed the Hydra in a chokehold at the top of its neck. I noticed Samuel and Makara were each busy with one of the heads, while Anna was behind the Hydra, dodging its swiping, spiky tail. She was trying to find an opening to stab it with her katana.

I screamed as the neck shook me loose, sending me spiraling horizontally through the air. Disoriented, I got up, only to knock my head on the creature's belly. I had somehow ended up underneath it.

But when my head hit it, I realized this part was soft. Taking my chance, I took out my gun and fired.

It clicked. The magazine was empty.

A head snaked under its body, searching me out. I scrambled away, reaching for my combat knife. It wasn't often that I used it. I hadn't had the need.

Until now.

I took it out, and stabbed the blade upward into the creature's gut.

It gave a horrible wail, and purple gunk spewed onto the floor, covering my legs. Disgusted, I drew back, but I couldn't stop. Infected or not, I had to keep gashing it. I stabbed it again and again. Its tail behind slashed wildly, nearly hitting Anna. She slid on the floor, through the puddle of goo, holding her katana up as she slid. The blade sliced through the stomach, making a deep wound – so deep that it couldn't support the creature's bowels, which tumbled out and plopped on the floor right in front of me.

The Hydra's legs gave out, and I had to move before it crushed me. I slid out of the way just as it came down, Anna doing the same thing on the creature's other side. It crashed to the floor. Its tentacle-like necks quivered and grew still.

I was covered with warm purple blood and monster excrement. I felt as if I could wash myself for the rest of time and never be clean.

"Gross does not even begin to describe this," I said.

"Come on," Samuel said. "Stairs are over here."

I followed the others, looking and smelling like death. We ran upstairs, and somehow, the monsters had gotten in. They chased us up through the flights. Looking down, I saw them two floors below us.

We were on floor twenty. We still had thirty to go.

I was exhausted, but I pushed myself onward. We took the steps two and three at a time, never letting up.

Finally, with ten floors left, Makara collapsed. The monsters were just one flight down. And unlike us, they didn't get tired.

"Come on!" I yelled. "Get up, let's go!"

I remembered all the times Makara had forced me to go on. It was my turn to return the favor.

I grabbed her with my fetid hand and pulled her up. Together, we ran the rest of the way. There were dozens of crawlers slithering their way upon their squat, bowed legs.

Finally, we made it to the tunnel that led to the runway door. The temperature up here was cold, and the monster fluids covering me from head to toe certainly didn't help matters. We ran at a sprint until the door came into view.

Unlatching it, Samuel pushed it open. The rush of subzero wind would freeze all the liquids on my body within moments. Crying out from the pain of it, I ran with the others across the runway, wondering why Ashton had told us to come here, and how long it would take us to die from either the monsters or the cold. There was nothing waiting for us, as the doctor had promised. There was only a sea of crawlers closing in from every direction. There was no airplane, helicopter, or anything else I had expected. Whatever was supposed to be here was not.

Monsters flooded the runway from all sides, including the door we'd left behind.

There were hundreds – maybe even thousands, of crawlers.

I had to admit the truth; we weren't going to get out of this one alive.

TWENTY-THREE

That was when a blinding light flew over the top of Cheyenne Mountain. And I mean, *flying*. The engine roared, drowning out even the noise of the monsters. Even they paused a bit at the approach of the giant, flying machine. The machine flew closer, along the side of the mountain from where it had been hidden, floodlights illuminating our shivering bodies on the runway.

It wasn't a plane – no plane could move like that.

"Is that a *ship?*" Anna asked.

I had little time to be surprised. The monsters regained their focus and closed in as the ship descended and hovered above us. Anna sliced a couple crawlers open as they neared, and the rest of us fired into the braver ones edging nearer. A porthole opened on the ship and a synthetic rope ladder descended.

"Go!" Samuel said to me.

I hopped on, scrambling upward to make room for the others. Anna came after me, then Makara. Finally, even with only one good arm, Samuel hopped up, forcing his legs up the ladder.

The ladder was unwieldy, swaying back and forth in the bitterly cold wind. I could no longer feel my fingers or toes.

Anna pushed me up from behind.

"Go, Alex!"

I forced myself to keep moving, but I couldn't keep it up for long. The cold was sapping it out of me.

It was all I could do to hold on as the ship lifted up from the ground. The monsters below closed around where we had been standing, howling at seeing their prey escape.

The ladder began retracting into the ship, carrying all of us with it.

Just hold on…

We neared the porthole. Finally, I entered it and was inside the ship, falling onto the cold deck. The others pulled themselves through and piled next to me. Samuel entered last, and then the porthole slid shut.

In the pitch black, the engines of the spaceship roared, and I felt it increase in speed.

I lay on the deck, shivering and cold. The ship hummed all around us.

"We made it," Makara said.

"Yeah," Samuel said. "Just barely."

"I guess we'll meet the doctor soon," Anna said.

As we sat there in the dark compartment, no one said anything. We only shivered and huddled together for warmth. The gunk on my clothes and skin had completely frozen from being outside for a mere two minutes, but it had done little about the smell.

A nearby door hissed open. We all turned toward the light, but no one appeared.

Then the man's voice came from the intercom.

"Step inside. It's warmer in here than the cargo bay. Welcome aboard the *Gilgamesh.*"

The intercom clicked off.

"Is this really a spaceship?" I asked.

"Looks like it," Samuel said.

"Did you read anything about *that* in your Black Files?"

"Nope."

Warm air gushed out of the door. That was enough incentive for me to stand and make my way forward. The others followed me. I stepped into the light, and the door hissed shut behind.

The surfaces were all gray. We went up a short set of steps, seeming to enter what appeared to be a central compartment, containing a table and several metallic doors leading out. A corridor extended directly ahead.

We walked forward, unsure of where we were going. The corridor was narrow, and we passed an open doorway on our left that revealed a clustered kitchen. On our right was a door that was shut, and on our left again was an open doorway, leading into what appeared to be a conference room.

The corridor went ninety degrees right for just a few feet before resuming its former course, where ahead I could see the opening to the bridge. Within I could see controls, LCD screens, and a pilot's seat. Above the rim of the seat was a head of wild, white hair, but the seat's back hid the man from view. The windshield was dark.

When we entered the bridge, the man remained seated. He then swiveled in his chair, revealing a wrinkled face, sharp blue eyes, and unkempt, white hair that descended to his shoulders. He wore khaki pants, a long-sleeved green shirt, and a thick brown vest.

"My God," he said, "you could have at least cleaned up a little before coming in here."

No one said anything. We were cold, exhausted, and had nearly died a dozen times in the past hour. We weren't exactly in the mood for humor.

At our silence, the man continued. "As you might

have guessed, I'm Dr. Cornelius Ashton. You can call me Ashton; it's not quite as bad as Cornelius. And this is the *Gilgamesh* – one of several advanced spaceships built by the U.S. government during the Dark Decade. It runs on a prototype miniature fusion reactor with a titanium and carbon nanotube alloy hull – light as a feather, but stronger by many factors than steel."

"And where are we going, in this spaceship?" Samuel asked.

"You must be Samuel," Ashton said. "You look just like your father." The man turned to Makara. "And you must be little Makara. Not so little, anymore. You were probably too young to remember me. And you two, I don't know."

"That would be Alex and Anna," Makara put in quickly. "And Lisa...Lisa is gone."

"I'm sorry to hear that," Ashton said. "But we don't have much time, in any sense. I can explain it all later. Right now, we need to get home."

"Home?" Samuel asked. "What do you mean?"

"You don't know about it yet," Ashton said, "but you will. This place was known to only to a few on the surface. I was one of those few, among the President and others." He pressed a button on the dash. *"Gilgamesh*...take us to Skyhome."

A deep, computerized male voice responded. "Destination: Skyhome."

The ship shifted below us, aiming upward.

"Strap yourselves in," Ashton said. "We'll be there in mere minutes."

"Skyhome," I said. "Is that a space station?"

"Yes. The Skyhome Program was the other side of the coin from the Bunkers. The government planned to build more – but funds ran out, so Skyhome was the only one ever completed. It was never populated; it served as a backup in case Bunker One fell."

"So the President is alive?" I asked.

"In a sense," Ashton said. "I'm one of the few survivors of Bunker One, and the highest ranking official, so technically, that would make me the President. But if you call me that, I might have to punch you. Now hurry up and strap yourselves in. The ship won't leave until you do."

We hurried to do as Ashton asked. By the time we were seated, the ship set itself in motion, pointing in a 45-degree angle upward.

"Here we go," Ashton said.

Suddenly, I was pushed back in my seat, and there were stars as we broke through the clouds. The ascent went on for several minutes, and all the while I could see the stars grow in intensity. A minute later, the ship slowed, and I felt myself floating up in my seat, restrained only by my safety harness.

We had escaped not only Bunker One, but Earth's gravity. The ship changed its trajectory, away from the countless stars, until the curved surface of Earth came into view. It was dark, shaded in night, and haloed by an aurora of violet blue. Straight ahead was the moon, unbelievably bright and clear without any of Earth's atmosphere to dim its grandeur. Countless stars studded the black void.

No one said anything as we were enthralled by the vista. It was hard to believe that this wasn't all a dream. When I was young, I thought I would go my whole life without ever riding in a car, much less a plane. Now, I was flying in a spaceship.

Surreal didn't even begin to describe it.

"That's...space," Makara said, the first to speak. "Outer space."

Ashton gave a small smile. "Yes. You'll get used to it, though. A few months out here you'll be longing for solid ground under your feet, I guarantee it."

We remained quiet as we continued on our course. Ten minutes later, a shape formed in the distance. Three rings of different sizes – a small one in the center, a medium one outside that, and the largest one on the periphery, spun around the central hub, out of which branched gleaming blue solar arrays. Flecks of green colored the windows of the outer ring – perhaps plants being grown?

"There it is," Ashton said with pride. "Skyhome."

Everyone found themselves at a complete loss for words. This Skyhome would be our chance to rest and recoup, and Ashton could tell us everything he knew about the xenovirus and the Voice.

But above all, I hoped there would be hot showers and hot food.

TWENTY-FOUR

There was nothing to do, but wait.

We had been in Skyhome for a full month, and it had taken me a week just to get used to the dizzy spinning of the stars from its three rotating rings. The fact that we were here, in space, never ceased to be mind-blowing.

Beginning in the Dark Decade, NASA devoted all of its energy to the Skyhome Program. Skyhome One was the only one to ever be completed, because even then it had taken ten years, hundreds of launches and several trillion dollars just to get it livable. Skyhome was designed to be self-sufficient, but in the rare case that a spare part or supply was needed, the *Gilgamesh* could easily travel between Skyhome and one of the Bunkers. *Odin*, a second, smaller ship, was also docked in Skyhome's hangar.

The *Gilgamesh*, as well as the *Odin*, had been constructed during the Dark Decade. An advanced, reusable spacecraft was commissioned by the government for the purpose of carrying supplies from the surface to Earth's orbit, while also having military applications to face the known alien threat. During the 2020s, huge advances were made in fusion power, giving a power supply that was more than enough to power spaceships far larger than anyone could have previously guessed.

Furthermore, quantum leaps in the field of carbon nanotube production allowed for lightweight hulls that could more than withstand the rigors of atmosphere reentry. Taken together, the United States was able to construct four spacecraft, each equipped with conventional smart missiles and twin machine gun turrets.

Though the fusion drive was massive, the enormous amount of energy it produced was more than enough to make up for it. To refuel, the ships would not need complex rocket fuel, a commodity that would not have existed for long post-Ragnarok. All they needed was hydrogen, the most abundant element in the universe.

Unfortunately, *Gilgamesh* and *Odin* were the only ships that were operational. The other two, *Orion* and *Perseus*, were still docked in Bunker Six, a massive complex not too far from Bunker One. Of course, it was covered with the Great Blight, so getting in and liberating the ships was extremely risky. Skyhome just did not have the manpower to do it.

In that first month at Skyhome, we finally got our chance to rest. We ate good food, grown and raised in the vast Outer Ring. The plants produced oxygen, and the humans and animals in turn produced carbon dioxide. All water was recycled within the closed environment, and there was plenty in reserve in case something went wrong. And, of course, the sunlight provided more than enough energy for both the electronics and plants.

Living in space, however, brought two great risks, and Skyhome had so far been spared from both. The first was radiation. While Skyhome had normally adequate radiation shielding, a sudden solar flare would douse the station with unhealthy levels of radiation, frying electronics as well as anyone exposed to the harmful rays. There was also the threat of stray rocks and debris striking the station. Skyhome had a tracking system that monitored space debris orbiting Earth, but the system wasn't perfect. There had been a couple times in Skyhome's history where its occupants had to do an emergency EVA to change the course of debris on a crash course with the station. If anything hit, it could potentially vent the station in mere minutes.

Getting hit by smaller debris was a somewhat common occurrence. Usually, the pieces were not large and fast enough to go through the station's shell, but if they were, there was a system in place within Skyhome that detected leaks. After the leak was discovered and pinpointed, it was a simple matter of sealing the hole with resin until a more permanent repair could be implemented.

But for now, Skyhome operated, and within its three rings people lived and worked. It was strange, seeing so many people again. About one hundred lived here, survivors of both Bunker One and Bunker Six. The entire community had reacted to our coming with a mixture of fascination and fear. The citizens of Skyhome treated us in much the same way as a Bunker resident would have treated a Wastelander. Sometimes, it felt as if we had been the subject of fear and speculation...perhaps even legend.

Among the survivors from Bunker One living in the station, none knew Samuel or Makara.

I spent a lot of my time tending the plants. They grew lots of different fruits and vegetables: potatoes, carrots, corn, wheat, tomatoes, broccoli, lettuce, cucumbers, apples, bananas, and many, many more. Unlike Bunker 108, live chickens provided meat and eggs.

We had countless questions of our own to ask of Dr.

Ashton, from how he had contacted us in the first place, to what to do about the coming invasion. The doctor said that resting and regaining our strength was more important for the moment. None of us argued with him there.

After the first couple of weeks, though, Anna was stewing. She practiced her forms, much as she had done before heading to Bunker One. Though we had nothing but time up here, she had somehow grown more distant from me. I think the journey to Bunker One had taken more of a toll than she let on.

If Anna had grown a bit more distant, Makara had grown light years away. She was still reeling from Lisa's death. Bunker One had been more than we all had bargained for, and it had cost us all something. But it cost Makara the most of all. Any attempt of mine to talk to her ended with her brushing me off. It got to the point where I just stopped trying, and ended up getting involved in my own activities.

I still felt the shock of it all. My life ever since Bunker 108 had been nonstop action; hunger, cold, being chased, and nearly getting killed hundreds of times. It had transformed me from an innocent kid into an adult, and with this newfound time, I could finally process everything. It was a transformation that was reflected in the mirror. I had been scrawny before, but since Bunker 108, I had gained a lot of muscle, especially since starting to recuperate at Skyhome. I ate constantly, used the weight room like it was my religion, and did sprints around the Outer Ring. I did a lot of sleeping – at least, if the nightmares didn't wake me. I started practicing hand-to-hand combat with Samuel once his sling was good to come off, and sometimes, Anna would teach me what she knew, when she wasn't busy.

I thought about my dad, Khloe, and everyone I had lost back in Bunker 108. It got to the point that I didn't even know who I was anymore. That was why I threw myself into my workouts, my reading, and my gardening. It was as if everyone had their own sorrows to deal with, and for a while, we just needed to be on our own. Maybe that was why Ashton wanted us to stay here awhile before continuing with our mission – whatever our mission was, these days.

As for Samuel, he and Ashton spoke every day, sometimes for hours. It made sense, because they were both scientists, and they were probably sharing information they had learned about the xenovirus. I hoped that they could come up with some idea of how to stop it. Every day, when I saw Samuel at dinner, I asked him what the next step was. He told me he'd tell us all when we were ready.

And Makara...she just stayed in her room, mostly. We did what we could to draw her out, but she wasn't biting. For some reason, she blamed herself for Lisa's death. She came out to eat, and she kept herself in shape as much as the rest of us, and took a job monitoring solar equipment. But she just wasn't there. It was saddening to see something finally breaking her, and it wasn't from the outside. It was from within. For some people, thinking isn't a good thing.

Resting in Skyhome was better than getting shot at or getting attacked by monsters, but it didn't feel like reality. Skyhome wasn't Earth, even if it was the best replication of Earth the United States could make with their limited resources. Here, I felt like a rat in a cage, and I was itching to get back, as crazy as that sounded. I remember Ashton's words, about longing to feel solid turf under my feet. I wanted more than that, though. I wanted the cold wind, the wide plains and mountains...

Skyhome was safe. But maybe safe wasn't exactly what I wanted anymore.

I *had* changed.

TWENTY-FIVE

The day finally came.

Ashton called us to his office. It was his first time meeting with all of us since Bunker One.

"At current expansion rates, the xenovirus will have taken everything over in twenty years," Ashton said. "At which point, the human race on the surface will most likely be extinct."

We stood silent as he faced us. Beyond the ports was the blue-green glow of Earth, swathed with pink and white clouds. Bright bands of stars streaked the cosmos. Ashton looked at each of us in turn.

"So, what do you want us to do about it?" I asked.

Ashton let the question fall to the wayside as he steepled his fingers. "With you and your team, I can finally get started on that."

"Get started on what?" Anna asked. "Why can't someone else in Skyhome do it?"

"Because no one in Skyhome is capable of what you guys have done," Ashton said. "You crossed the Great Blight, raided Bunker One, and retrieved the Black Files – among other things, I'm sure. No one here could have done as much. None of us would have dared to do it, because we all *knew* just how bad it was. You and your team have been on the surface and have survived there for years. No one here has that kind of experience. In short, I *need* you. The world needs you. You are the only people who even have a *shot* of pulling off what I have in mind."

Anna sighed. "No pressure, then."

"Before you go on, there's something I need to know," I asked. "Was it you who opened the door to Bunker 40?"

Ashton nodded. "I heard your voices through the camera there. While I could not communicate with you, I heard you clearly. I keep tabs on all the Bunkers that are still connected to Skyhome, and if anything unusual happens, it's usually good about letting me know. When you mentioned Chief Security Officer Chan, the xenovirus, and the Black Files, I decided to open the door. The Imperials had been trying the same thing for months, but I wasn't going to let them in. I just hoped you guys would come out ahead in that situation."

"What about the plane?" I asked. "Were you controlling that as well?"

"I didn't control the plane, though its course to Bunker One was plotted through Skyhome's navigational system. I knew as long as you guys made it to the Bunker One labs, I could radio you there."

"Was there not a radio on the plane?" I asked.

"There was," Ashton said. "Unfortunately, I could not figure out how to contact you, as much as I tried. The radio in my lab at Bunker One – I *do* know how to communicate with that. The Imperials got there first, however. I couldn't open those doors until they were dealt with."

Makara turned her head away. The deaths of

Harland and Drake had cost Lisa her life, and that fact wasn't lost on any of us.

Ashton paused, as if to collect his thoughts. "Rather than surprise you all with my voice while you were reading the Black Files, which would have distracted you, I instead rushed to upgrade Samuel's clearance remotely so that he would have no trouble accessing them. I waited, and listened to your conversation, hoping that Samuel would explain everything adequately. I was prepared to fill in any missing information, but he explained it all rather well.

"However, it became clear that you could not remain in Bunker One long. Skyhome's surface monitors intercepted a sound wave from Ragnarok Crater indicating that the swarm was on the move. That was when I spoke to you all, from this very office, warning you to get to the runway. After that, I rushed to the *Gilgamesh*. I could be at Bunker One within thirty minutes. I didn't think you would have that amount of time. Turns out, though...I made it just in time."

"And now we're here," I said.

"Quite the story," Makara said.

"Indeed," Ashton said. "But now that we're all here, and you know how you came to *be* here, we can focus on what needs to be done. You've had a month to rest and gain a sense of normalcy in your lives, such as normalcy counts. We must plan for the future."

"What do you mean?" I asked.

"Xenofall is coming," Ashton said. "And you are going to be the ones who stop it."

"How?" I asked.

Samuel turned to face us. "Back in Bunker One, I talked about there being a central hub that communicates with the xenofungal network. Ashton came up with much the same idea, and we think there might be something to it. However, we can't know anything unless we have feet on the ground."

"You need someone to investigate Ragnarok Crater, don't you?" I asked.

Samuel nodded. "That's right. The only thing is it's the oldest part of the Great Blight. The monsters will be thickest there, especially if there is some sort of central hub controlling everything. They'll want to protect it."

"What makes you think there *is* a central hub?" Anna asked.

"The question isn't '*is* there one?'" Dr. Ashton said. "It's a question of *where* it is. The wavelength monitor picks up a frequency coming from the Crater, so that's where it is. The question is getting there to destroy it."

"And what will it look like?" I asked. "Is it a brain, or something else?"

"We don't know," Samuel said. "That's what we need to find out."

"So how do we get in there without being seen?" I asked.

"There's probably no way to get in there without being seen," Samuel said. "It'll be an all-out battle."

"There's four of us," I said, "and you want us to fight a battle against *everything?* I don't think so."

"That's where the first part of our mission comes in," Samuel said. "We'll need reinforcements."

"And where are we to find these reinforcements?" Anna asked.

"Down there," Samuel said, pointing to Earth. "We have two spaceships up here, the *Gilgamesh* and the *Odin*. We can take *Odin*."

"Who's going to fly it?" Makara asked.

"You are," Ashton said. "You have quick reflexes, and from what I hear, you did a great job piloting the Recon. A spaceship is different, obviously, but I suspect you might have a knack for it."

Makara's eyes widened. It was the first time I'd seen them light up in weeks. "I could learn that."

"There are still a few things we need to take care of," Samuel said. "Number one is stopping the war between the Empire and Raider Bluff. This will mean contacting both Char and Augustus. We'll need both if we're going to take the fight to Ragnarok. We also need to locate Bunkers 76 and 88. Along with soldiers, we'll want their weapons and supplies. And it would be good to find out if they're still around."

"Okay," I said, "stop a war and find a couple Bunkers. Should be easy."

"We should also go to L.A. and Vegas, too," Samuel said. "It's a long shot, but they are the most populous cities in America at the moment. If we can get any of the gangs interested, they could join us in the attack."

"They'll be too busy fighting each other for that," Anna said.

"We have to try," Samuel said. "I'm sure they're worried about the Blights as well. Who wouldn't be? When we propose a plan that could destroy the Blights, they'll listen."

"How will we get everyone to the Crater?" I asked. *"Odin,* from what I understand, is smaller than *Gilgamesh,* and even *Gilgamesh* and *Odin* together wouldn't be big enough to transport everyone. Not by a long shot."

Ashton answered. "I've calculated that both ships together can carry well over a hundred passengers. It'll be like sardines, but it could be done, no problem."

"So we board both ships with a strike team of the very best," Samuel said. "Meanwhile, the vast majority of the army will enter the Great Blight from the southwest, near where we entered it. Hopefully, that move will draw the attention of the Voice, and with luck, the Great Blight's interior will be left undefended. That's when we drop in, find the hub that controls the Voice, and destroy it."

"*Alleged* hub," Makara said. "We still have no idea if it exists or not."

"It does," Ashton said. "Something is behind the Voice. If that can be destroyed, the entire invasion will be directionless. It is something we must do before the second wave comes."

"And when is that?"

Ashton paused. "I don't know. I'm listening for any sign of the coming invasion, but so far, there has been nothing. Worse, we can't predict their numbers, or what fighting capacity they'll have." He paused. "In the meantime, *Odin* is all yours. *Gilgamesh* will remain here with me. I have my own errands to run."

"How long until I can pilot it?" Makara asked.

"There's not much to it, actually," Ashton said. "I learned the controls within a month. It's what you do with that training that counts. In the interim, everyone continue to recover while Makara trains."

We had our work cut out for us. We would know, very soon, which of us would be extinct: us, or *them*. After seeing what the xenovirus could do, the odds didn't seem to be in our favor.

Xenofall was coming.

THE END OF BOOK TWO

Now available:
EVOLUTION
The third book of *The Wasteland Chronicles* by
Kyle West

To stop the virus, enemies must become friends.

After two months in Skyhome, Alex and the crew are

rested and healed from their ordeal in Bunker One. But the war against the xenovirus is only beginning.

They must leave the safety of the space station to gain the favor of Emperor Augustus of Nova Roma. But when disaster strikes outside the capital, the team must scramble to save one of their own.

It's a fight that pits them against the Empire's finest. But even Nova Roma isn't immune to the xenovirus or its newest evolutions...

ABOUT THE AUTHOR

Kyle West is the author of *The Wasteland Chronicles* and *Xenoworld Saga* series, as well as a new science fiction series set for release in late 2020.

From a young age, he's enjoyed just about anything science fiction or fantasy, with a particular fascination for end-of-the-world scenarios. His goal is to write as many entertaining books as possible, with interesting worlds and characters that hopefully give his readers a break from the mundane.

He truly appreciates his readers, and invites them to connect with him through his Facebook page, website, or mailing list.

kylewestwriter.com

facebook.com/kylewestwriter

goodreads.com/kylewest

GLOSSARY

10,000, The: This refers to the 10,000 citizens who were selected in 2029 to enter Bunker One. This group included the best America had to offer, people who were masters in the fields of science, engineering, medicine, and security. President Garland and all the U.S. Congress, as well as essential staff and their families, were chosen.

Alpha: "Alpha" is the title given to the recognized head of the Raiders. In the beginning, it was merely a titular role that only had as much power as the Alpha was able to enforce. But as Raider Bluff grew in size and complexity, the Alpha took on a more meaningful role. Typically, Alphas do not remain so for long – they are assassinated by rivals who rise to take their place. In some years, there can be as many as four Alphas – though powerful Alphas, like Char, can reign for many years.

Batts: Batts, or batteries, are the currency of the Wasteland and the Empire. They are accepted anywhere that the Empire's caravans reach. It is unknown *how* batteries were first seen as currency, but it is rumored that Augustus himself instigated the policy. Using them as currency makes sense: batteries are small, portable, and durable, and have the intrinsic quality of being useful. Rechargeable batteries (called "chargers") are even more prized, and solar batteries (called "solars," or "sols") are the most useful and prized of all.

Behemoth: The Behemoth is a great monstrosity in the Wasteland – a giant creature, either humanoid or reptilian, or sometimes a mixture of the two, that can reach heights of ten feet or greater. They are bipedal, powerful, and can keep pace with a moving vehicle. All but the most powerful of guns are useless against the Behemoth's armored hide.

Black Reapers, The: The Black Reapers are a powerful, violent gang, based in Los Angeles. They are led by Warlord Carin Black. They keep thousands of slaves, using them to serve their post-apocalyptic empire. They usurped the Lost Angels in 2055, and have been ruling there ever since.

Black Files, The: The Black Files are the mysterious collected research on the xenovirus, located in Bunker One. They were authored principally by Dr. Cornelius Ashton, Chief Scientist of Bunker One.

Blights: Blights are infestations of xenofungus and the xenolife they support. They are typically small, but the bigger ones can cover large tracts of land. As a general rule of thumb, the larger the Blight, the more complicated and dangerous the ecosystem it maintains. The largest known Blight is the Great Blight – which covers a large portion of the central United States. Its center is Ragnarok Crater.

Boundless, The: The Boundless is an incredibly dry part of the Wasteland, ravaged by canyons and dust storms, situated in what used to be Arizona and New Mexico. Very little can survive in the Boundless, and no one is known to have ever crossed it.

Bunker 40: Bunker 40 is located on the outer fringes of the Great Blight in Arizona. It is hidden beneath a top-secret research facility, a vestige of the Old World. Many aircraft were stationed at Bunker 40 before it fell, sometime in the late 2050s.

Bunker 108: Bunker 108 is located in the San Bernardino Mountains about one hundred miles east of Los Angeles. It is the birthplace of Alex Keener.

Bunker 114: Bunker 114 is a medical research installation built about fifty miles northwest of Bunker 108. Built beneath Cold Mountain, Bunker 114 is small. After the fall of Bunker One, Bunker 114, like Bunker 108 to the southeast, became a main center of xenoviral research. An outbreak of the human strain of the xenovirus caused the Bunker to fall in 2060. Bunker 108's fall followed soon thereafter.

Bunker One: Bunker One was the main headquarters of the Post-Ragnarok United States government. It fell in 2048 to a swarm of crawlers that overran its defenses. Bunker One had berths for ten thousand people, making it many times over the most populous Bunker. Its inhabitants included President Garland, the U.S. Senate and House of Representatives, essential government staff, and security forces, along with the skilled people needed to maintain it. Also, dozens of brilliant scientists and specialists lived and worked there, including engineers, doctors, and technicians. The very wealthy were also allowed berths for helping to finance the Bunker Program. Bunker One is the location of the Black Files, authored by Dr. Cornelius Ashton.

Bunker Six: Bunker Six is a large installation located north of Bunker One, within driving distance. It houses the S-Class spaceships constructed during the Dark Decade – including *Gilgamesh*, the capital ship, and three smaller cruisers – *Odin*, *Perseus*, and *Orion*. While *Gilgamesh* and *Odin* are under Cornelius Ashton's care,

Perseus and *Orion* are still locked inside the fallen Bunker.

Bunker Program, The: The United States and Canadian governments pooled resources to establish 144 Bunkers in Twelve Sectors throughout their territory. The Bunkers were the backup in case the Guardian Missions failed. When the Guardian Missions *did* fail, the Bunker Program kicked into full gear. The Bunkers were designed to save all critical government personnel and citizenry, along with anyone who could provide the finances to construct them. The Bunkers were designed to last indefinitely, using hydroponics to grow food. The Bunkers ran on fusion power, which had been made efficient by the early 2020s. The plan was that, when the dust settled, Bunker residents could reemerge and rebuild. Most Bunkers fell, however, for various reasons – including critical systems failures, mutinies, and attacks by outsiders (see **Wastelanders**). By the year 2060, only four Bunkers were left.

Chaos Years, The: The Chaos Years refer to the ten years following the impact of Ragnarok. These dark years signified the great die-off of most forms of life, including humans. Most deaths occurred due to starvation. With mass global cooling, crops could not grow in climates too far from the tropics. What crops *would* grow produced a yield far too small to feed the population that existed. This led to a period of violence unknown in all of human history. The Chaos Years signify the complete breakdown of the Old World's remaining infrastructures – including food production, economies, power grids, and the industrial complex – all of which led to the deaths of billions of people.

Coleseo Imperio: *El Coleseo Imperio*, translated as the Imperial Coliseum, is a circular, three-tiered stone arena rising from the center of the city of Nova Roma, the capital of the Nova Roman Empire. It is used to host gladiatorial games in the tradition of ancient Rome, and serves as the chief sport of the Empire. Slaves and convicts are forced to fight in death matches, which serves the dual purpose of entertaining the masses while getting rid of prisoners and slaves who would otherwise be, in the Empire's eyes, liabilities. Ritual sacrifices routinely take place on the arena floor.

Crawlers: Crawlers are dangerous, highly mobile monsters spawned by Ragnarok. Their origin is unclear, but they share many characteristics of Earth animals – mostly those reptilian in nature, although other forms are more similar to insects. Crawlers are sleek and fast, and can leap through the air at very high speeds. Typically, crawlers attack in groups, and behave as if of one mind. One crawler will, without hesitation, sacrifice itself in order to reach its prey. Crawlers are especially dangerous when gathered in high numbers – at which point there is not much one can do but run. Crawlers can be killed, their weak points being their belly and their three eyes.

Dark Decade, The: The Dark Decade lasted from 2020-2030, from the time of the first discovery of Ragnarok, to the time of its impact. It is not called the Dark Decade because the world descended into madness immediately upon the discovery of Ragnarok by astronomer Neil Weinstein – that only happened in 2028, with the failure of *Messiah,* the third and last of the Guardian Missions. In the United States and other industrialized nations, life proceeded in an almost normal fashion. There were plenty of good reasons to believe that Ragnarok could be stopped, especially when given ten years. But as the Guardian Missions failed, one by one, the order of the world quickly disintegrated.

With the failure of the Guardian Mission *Archangel* in 2024, a series of wars engulfed the world. As what some were calling World War III embroiled the planet, the U.S. and several of its European allies, and Canada, continued to work on stopping Ragnarok. When the second Guardian Mission, *Reckoning*, failed, an economic depression swept the world. But none of this compared to the madness that followed upon the failure of the third and final Guardian, *Messiah*, in 2028. As societies broke down, martial law was enforced. President Garland was appointed dictator of the United States with absolute authority. By 2029, several states had broken off from the Union.

In the last quarter of 2030, an odd silence hung over the world, as if it had grown weary of living. The President, all essential governmental staff and military, the Senate and House of Representatives, along with scientists, engineers, and the talented and the wealthy, entered the 144 Bunkers established by the Bunker Program. Outraged, the tens of millions of people who did not get an invitation found the Bunker locations, demanding to be let in. The military took action when necessary.

Then, on December 3, 2030, Ragnarok fell, crashing into the border of Wyoming and Nebraska, forming a crater one hundred miles wide. The world left the Dark Decade, and entered the Chaos Years.

Flyers: Flyers are birds infected with the xenovirus. They fly in large swarms of a hundred or more. They are only common around large Blights, or within the Great Blight itself. The high metabolism of flyers means they cannot venture far from xenofungus, their main source of food. They are highly dangerous, and cannot be fought easily, because they fly in such large numbers.

Gilgamesh: *Gilgamesh* is an S-Class Capital Spaceship constructed by the United States during the Dark Decade. It holds room for twelve crewmen, thirteen counting the captain. Its fuselage is mostly made of carbon nanotubes – incredibly lightweight, and many, many times stronger than steel. It is powered by a proto-typical miniature fusion reactor, using deuterium and tritium as fuel. Its design is described as insect-like in appearance, for invisibility to radar. The ship contains a bridge, armory, conference room, kitchen, galley, two lavatories, a clinic, and twelve bunks for crew in two separate dorms. A modest captain's quarters can be reached from the galley, complete with its own lavatory. Within the galley is access to a spacious cargo bay, where supplies, and even a vehicle as large as a Recon, can be stored. The Recon can be driven off the ship's wide boarding ramp when grounded (this capability is the main difference between *Odin* and *Gilgamesh*...in addition to the cargo bay boarding ramp, *Gilgamesh* also contains a passenger's boarding ramp on the side, that also leads into the galley). The porthole has a retractable rope ladder that is good for up to five hundred feet. *Gilgamesh* has a short wingspan, but receives most of its lift from the four thrusters mounted in back, thrusters that have a wide arc of rotation that allows the ship to fly in almost any direction. The ship can go weeks without needing to refuel. As far as combat capabilities, *Gilgamesh* was primarily constructed as a reconnaissance and transport vessel. That said, it has twin machine gun turrets that open from beneath the ship. When grounded, it is supported by three struts, one in front, two in back.

Great Blight, The: The Great Blight is the largest xenofungal infestation in the world, its point of origin being Ragnarok Crater on the Great Plains in eastern Wyoming and western Nebraska. Unlike other Blights, the Great Blight is massive. From 2040-2060, it began to rapidly expand outside Ragnarok Crater at an alarming rate, moving as much as a quarter mile each day (meaning the stretching of the xenofungus could actually be discerned with the naked eye). Any and all life was conquered, killed, or acquired into the Great Blight's xenoparasitic network. Here, the first monsters were created. Animals would become ensnared in sticky pools of purple goo, and their DNA absorbed and preserved. The Great Blights, obeying some sort of consciousness, would then mix and match the DNA of varying species, tweaking and mutating the genes until, from the same pools it had acquired the DNA, it would give birth to new life forms, designed only to spread the Blight and kill whoever, or whatever, opposed that spreading. As time went on and the Xeno invasion became more sophisticated, the Great Blight's capabilities became advanced enough to direct the evolution of xenolife itself, leading to the creation of the xenovirus, meaning it could infect species far outside of the Blight – including, eventually, humans.

Guardian Missions: The Guardian Missions were humanity's attempts to intercept and alter the course of Ragnarok during the Dark Decade. There were three, and in the order they were launched, they were called *Archangel*, *Reckoning*, and *Messiah* (all three of which were also the names of the ships launched). Each mission had a reason for failing. *Archangel* is reported to have crashed into Ragnarok, in 2024. In 2026, *Reckoning* somehow got off-course, losing contact with Earth in the process. In 2028 *Messiah* successfully landed and attached its payload of rockets to the surface of Ragnarok in order to alter its course from Earth. However, the rockets failed before they had time to do their work. The failure of the Guardian Missions kicked the Bunker Program into overdrive.

Howlers: Howlers are the newest known threat posed by the xenovirus. They are human xenolife, and they behave very much like zombies. They attack with sheer numbers, using their bodies as weapons. A bite from a Howler is enough to infect the victim with the human strain of the xenovirus. Post-infection, it takes anywhere from a few minutes to a few hours for a corpse to reanimate into the dreaded howler. Worse, upon death, Howlers somehow explode, raining purple goo on anyone within range. Even if a little bit of goo enters the victim's bloodstream, he or she is as good as dead, cursed to become a Howler within a matter of minutes or hours. How the explosion occurs, no one knows – it is surmised that the xenovirus itself creates some sort of agent that reacts violently with water or some other fluid present within the Howlers. There is also reason to believe that certain Howlers become Behemoths, as was the case with Kari in Bunker 114.

Hydra: A powerful spawning of the xenovirus, the Hydra has only been seen deep in the heart of Bunker One. It contains three heads mounted on three stalk-like necks. It is covered in thick scales that serve as armor. It has a powerful tail that it can swing, from the end of which juts a long, cruel spike. It is likely an evolved, more deadly form of the crawler.

Ice Lands, The: Frozen in a perpetual blanket of ice and snow, the northern and southern latitudes of the planet are completely unlivable. In the Wasteland, at least, they are referred to as the Ice Lands. Under a blanket of meteor fallout, extreme global cooling was instigated in 2030. While the glaciers are only now experiencing rapid regrowth, they will advance for centuries to come until the fallout has dissipated enough to produce a warmer climate. In the Wasteland, 45 degrees north marks the beginning of what is considered the Ice Lands.

L.A. Gangland: L.A. Gangland means a much different thing than it did Pre-Ragnarok. In the ruins of Los Angeles, there are dozens of gangs vying for control, but by 2060, the most powerful is the Black Reapers, who usurped that title from the Lost Angels.

Lost Angels, The: The Lost Angels were post-apocalyptic L.A.'s first super gang. From the year 2050 until 2055, they reigned supreme in the city, led by a charismatic figure named Dark Raine. The Angels were different from other gangs – they valued individual freedom and abhorred slavery. Under the Angels' rule, Los Angeles prospered. The Angels were eventually usurped in 2056 by a gang called the Black Reapers, led by a man named Carin Black.

Nova Roma: Nova Roma is the capital of the Nova Roman Empire. It existed Pre-Ragnarok as a small town situated in an idyllic valley, flanked on three sides by green mountains. This town was also home to Augustus's palatial mansion – and it was around this mansion that the city that would one day rule the Empire had its beginnings. Over thirty years, as the Empire gained wealth and power under Augustus's rule, Nova Roma grew from a small village into a mighty city with a population numbering in the tens of thousands. Using knowledge of ancient construction techniques found in American Bunkers, Augustus employed talented engineers and thousands of slaves to build the city from the ground up. Inspired by the architecture of ancient Rome, some of the most notable construction projects in Nova Roma include the *Coleseo Imperio,* the Senate House, the Grand Forum, and Central Square. An aqueduct carries water over the city walls from the Sierra Madre Mountains north of the city. The city grows larger each passing year, so much so that shantytowns have overflowed its walls, attracted by the city's vast wealth.

Nova Roman Empire, The: The Nova Roman Empire (also known as the "Empire") is a collection of allied city-states that are ruled from Nova Roma, its capital in what was formerly the Mexican state of Guerrero. The Empire began as the territory of a Mexican drug cartel named the Legion. Through the use of brutal force, they kept security within their borders even as other governments fell.

Following the impact of Ragnarok, many millions of Americans fled south to escape the cold, dry climate that permeated northern latitudes. Mexico still remained warm, especially southern Mexico, and new global wind currents caused by Ragnarok kept Mexico clearer of meteor fallout than other areas of the world. At the close of the Chaos Years, Mexico was far more populous than the United States. Many city-states formed in the former republic, but most developed west of the Sierra Madre Mountains. Language clashes between native Mexicans and migrant Americans produced new dialects of both Spanish and English. Though racial tensions exist in the Empire, as Americans' descendants are the minority within it, Americans and their descendants are protected under law and are entitled to the same rights – at least in theory. The reality is, most refugees that entered Imperial territory were American – and most refugees ended up as slaves.

Of the hundreds of city-states that formed in Mexico, one was called Nova Roma, located inland in a temperate valley not too far east of Acapulco. Under the direction of the man styling himself as Augustus Imperator, formerly known as Miguel Santos, lord of the Legion drug cartel, the city of Nova Roma allied with neighboring city-states. Incorporating both Ancient Roman governmental values and Aztec mythology, the Empire expanded through either the conquest or annexation of rival city-states. By 2060, the Empire had hundreds of cities in its thrall, stretching from Oaxaca in the southeast all the way to Jalisco in the northwest. The Empire had also formed colonies as far north as Sonora, even founding a city called Colossus at the mouth of the

Colorado River, intended to be the provincial capital from which the Empire hoped to rule California and the Mojave.

Because of its size and power, the Empire is difficult to control. Except for its center, ruled out of Nova Roma, most of the city-states are autonomous and are only required to pay tribute and soldiers when called for during the Empire's wars. In the wake of the Empire's rapid conquests, Augustus developed the Imperial Road System in order to facilitate trade and communication, mostly done by horse. In an effort to create a unifying culture for the Empire, Emperor Augustus instigated a representative government, where all of Nova Roma's provinces have representation in the Imperial Senate. Augustus encouraged a universal religion based on Aztec mythology, whose gods are placed alongside the saints of Catholicism in the Imperial Pantheon. Augustus also instigated gladiatorial games, ordering that arenas be built in every major settlement of his Empire. This included the construction of dozens of arenas, including *El Coleseo Imperio* in Nova Roma itself, a large arena which, while not as splendid as the original Coliseum in Old Rome, is still quite impressive. The *Coleseo* can seat ten thousand people. By 2060, Augustus had accomplished what might have taken a century to establish otherwise.

Oasis: Oasis is a settlement located in the Wasteland, about halfway between Los Angeles and Raider Bluff. It has a population of one thousand, and is built around the banks of the oasis for which it is named. The oasis did not exist Pre-Ragnarok, but was formed by tapping an underground aquifer. Elder Ohlan rules Oasis with a strong hand. He is the brother of Dark Raine, and it is whispered that he might have had a hand in his death.

Odin: *Odin* is an S-Class Cruiser Spaceship built by

the U.S. during the Dark Decade. It is one of four, the other being *Gilgamesh,* the capital ship, and the other two being *Perseus* and *Orion,* cruisers with the same specs as *Odin.* Though *Odin's* capabilities are not as impressive as *Gilgamesh's, Odin* is still very functional. It contains berths for eight crew, nine counting the captain. It has a cockpit, armory, kitchen, galley, two dorms, one lavatory, and the fusion drive in the aft. A cargo bay can be reached from either outside the ship or within the galley. Unlike *Gilgamesh,* it is not spacious enough to store a Recon. It contains a single machine gun turret that can open up from the ship's bottom. *Odin,* in addition to being faster than *Gilgamesh,* also gets better fuel efficiency. It can go months without needing to refuel.

Praetorians, The: The Praetorians are the most elite of the Empire's soldiers. There are one hundred total, and they are the personal bodyguard of Emperor Augustus. They carry a long spear, tower shield, and gladius. They wear a long, purple cape, steel armor, and a white jaguar headdress, complete with purple plume. They are also trained in the use of guns.

Raider Bluff: Raider Bluff is the only known settlement of the raiders. It is built northeast of what used to be Needles, California, on top of a three-tiered mesa. Though the raiders are a mobile group, even they need a place to rest during the harsh Wasteland winter. Merchants, women, and servants followed the Raider men, setting up shop on the mesa, giving birth to Raider Bluff sometime in the early 2040s. From the top of the Bluff rules the Alpha, the strongest recognized leader of the Raiders. A new Alpha rises only when he is able to wrest control from the old one.

Ragnarok: Ragnarok was the name given the meteor that crashed into Earth on December 3, 2030. It was about three miles long, and two miles wide. It was discovered by astronomer Neil Weinstein, in 2019. It is not known *what* caused Ragnarok to come hurtling toward Earth, or how it eluded detection for so long – but that answer was revealed when the Black Files came to light. Ragnarok was the first phase of the invasion planned by the Xenos, the race of aliens attempting to conquer Earth. Implanted within Ragnarok was the xenovirus – the seed for all alien genetic life that was to destroy, acquire, and replace Earth life. The day the Xenos arrive, according to the Black Files, is called "Xenofall." The time of their eventual arrival is completely unknown.

Ragnarok Crater: Ragnarok Crater is the site of impact of the meteor Ragnarok. It is located on the border of Wyoming and Nebraska, and is about one hundred miles wide with walls eight miles tall. It's the center of the Great Blight, and it is also the origin of the Voice, the consciousness that directs the behavior of all xenolife.

Recon: A Recon is an all-terrain rover that is powered by hydrogen. It is designed for speedy recon missions across the Wastes, and was developed by the United States military during the Dark Decade. It is composed of a cab in front, and a large cargo bay in the back. Mounted on top of the cargo bay is a turret with 360-degree rotation, accessible by a ladder and a port-hole. The turret can be manned and fired while the Recon is on the go.

Skyhome: Skyhome is a three-ringed, self-sufficient space station constructed by the United States during the Dark Decade, designed to house two hundred and fifty people. Like the Bunkers, it contains its own power, hydroponics, and water reclamation system designed to keep the station going as long as possible. Skyhome was never actually occupied until 2048, after the falls of both Bunker One and Bunker Six. Cornelius Ashton assumed control of the station, along with survivors from both

Bunkers, in order to continue his research on the xenovirus which had destroyed his entire life.

Voice, The: The Voice is the name given to the collective consciousness of all xenolife. It exists in Ragnarok Crater – whether or not it has a corporeal form is unknown. However, it is agreed by Dr. Ashton and Samuel that the Voice controls xenolife using sound waves and vibrations within xenofungus. The Voice also sends sound waves that can be detected by xenolife while off the xenofungus. The Voice gives the entire Xeno invasion sentience, and is a piece of evidence pointing to an advanced alien race that is trying to conquer Earth.

Wanderer, The: A blind prophet who wanders the Wasteland, of mysterious origin.

Wastelanders: Wastelanders are surface dwellers, specifically ones that live in the southwestern United States. The term is broad – it can be as specific as to mean only someone who is forced to wander, scavenge, or raid for sustenance, or Wastelander can mean anyone who lives on the surface Post-Ragnarok, regardless of location or circumstances. Wastelanders are feared by Bunker dwellers, as they have been the number one reason for Bunkers failing.

Wasteland, The: The Wasteland is a large tract of land comprised of Southern California and the adjacent areas of the Western United States. It extends from the San Bernardino Mountains in the west, to the Rockies in the east (and in later years, the Great Blight), and from the northern border of Nova Roma on the south, to the Ice Lands to the north (which is about the same latitude as Sacramento, California). The Wasteland is character-ized by a cold, extremely dry climate. Rainfall each year is little to none, two to four inches being about average. Little can survive the Wasteland, meaning that all life has clung to limited water supplies. Major population centers include Raider Bluff, along the Colorado River; Oasis, supplied by a body of water of the same name; and Last Town, a trading post that sprung up along I-10 between Los Angeles and the Mojave. Whenever the Wasteland is referred to, it is generally not referred to in its entire scope. It is mainly used to reference what was once the Mojave Desert.

Xenodragon: The xenodragon is the newest manifestation of the xenovirus. It is very much like a dragon – reptilian, lightweight, with colossal wings that provide it with both lift and speed. There are different kinds of xenodragons, but the differences are little known, other than whether they are large or small. A particularly large xenodragon makes its roost on Raider Bluff.

Xenofall: Xenofall is the day of reckoning – when the Xenos finally arrive on Earth to claim it as their own. No one knows when that day is – whether it is in one year, ten years, or a thousand. It is feared that, when Xenofall *does* come, humans and all resistance will have been long gone.

Xenofungus: Xenofungus is a slimy, sticky fungus that is colored pink, orange, or purple (and sometimes all three), that infests large tracts of land and serves as the chief food source of all xenolife. It forms the basis of the Blights, and without xenofungus, xenolife could not exist. The fungus, while hostile to Earth life, facilitates the growth, development, and expansion of xenolife. It is nutrient-rich, and contains complicated compounds and proteins that are poison to Earth life, but ambrosia for xenolife. It is tough, resilient, resistant to fire, dryness, and cold – and if it isn't somehow stopped, one day xenofungus will cover the entire world.

Xenolife: Any form of life that is infected with the xenovirus.

Xenomind: A Xenomind is an ancient sentient being, evolved over the eons by the xenovirus and xenofungus. They are split into two factions – the *Radaskim* and the *Elekai*. The *Radaskim* are warlike and want to conquer all life in the universe – a seemingly impossible aim. The *Elekai* want to stop the *Radaskim* from achieving this. So far, on every world the Eternal War has been fought, the *Elekai* have lost.

Xenovirus: The xenovirus is an agent that acquires genes, adding them to its vast collection. It then mixes and matches the genes under its control to create something completely new, whether a plant, animal, bacteria, etc. There are thousands of strains of the xenovirus, maybe even millions, but most are completely undocumented. While the underlying core of each strain is the same, the strains are specific to each species it infects. Failed strains completely drop out of existence, but the successful ones live on. The xenovirus was first noted by Dr. Cornelius Ashton of Bunker One. His collected research on the xenovirus was compiled in the Black Files, which were lost in the fall of Bunker One in 2048.

ALSO BY KYLE WEST

The Wasteland Chronicles

Apocalypse

Origins

Evolution

Revelation

Darkness

Extinction

Xenofall

The Xenoworld Saga

Prophecy

Bastion

Beacon

Sanctum

Kingdom

Dissolution

Aberration

Standalone

Lost Angel (Prequel)